Kitsu's Diary is bold, honest, direct, and true to life. There is a gripping element to this story as we helplessly watch Kitsu slip into the age-old trap of love before its time. The description of her inner life through the diary is an excellent device for a young girl and it works well. Also, suffering with her through the consequences is rife with conviction and ministry power.

All in all, I think it's a winner that could potentially reach lots of young girls.

Fred Rubi, Senior Pastor, Potters House Church, South London

Kitsu's range of emotions in falling for Trevor shows just how complex being in love can be. It also shows just how one emotion (love) can overpower a blend of other emotions (fear, confusion, pain, resentment, jealousy, anger, envy). Emotions that, under other circumstances, would cause the individual to pause and reconsider, but in this case are incapacitated, rendering the "victim" wilfully self-deceived by "love."

Desiri has a wonderful ability to paint a vivid picture of individuals, their circumstances, and the range of emotions they go through. As a result, she shares a story that grips you from the very beginning, as you want to know more about Kitsu, her world, and where her world would lead. I was immediately sucked into the story, fascinated by Kitsu. It was as if I was with her in her journey and through Desiri's writing, able to connect to her, as if she was a real person; as if I knew her.

I would encourage everyone to read this book and join Kitsu on her journey too.

Jay Nembhard, Pastor, Potters House Church, South London

I enjoyed reading this book, it covers a lot of things that young girls go through nowadays. It is also a wake-up call for anyone going through this type of situation; it opens up greater doors for them to know that they're not alone. When you have published this book, someone needs to find it and turn it into a movie or a TV series. I would watch it.

Joy Okobia, Student, Aged 15

Kitsu's
DIARY

The Things I
Wish I Knew
When I was
Fifteen

DESIRI OKOBIA

WESTBOW
PRESS®
A DIVISION OF THOMAS NELSON
& ZONDERVAN

WestBow Press books may be ordered through booksellers or by contacting:

WestBow Press
A Division of Thomas Nelson & Zondervan
1663 Liberty Drive
Bloomington, IN 47403
www.westbowpress.com
1 (866) 928-1240

Scripture taken from the New King James Version®. Copyright © 1982 by Thomas Nelson. Used by permission. All rights reserved.

ISBN: 978-1-9736-9566-0 (sc)
ISBN: 978-1-9736-9567-7 (e)

Print information available on the last page.

WestBow Press rev. date: 08/26/2020

Contents

Dedication

For Jesus
and the generation that *will* make a difference.

Acknowledgments

God, because divine inspiration transforms
good works into masterpieces.

I also thank my Pastors, my family and my friends
who have supported me on this journey.

May God Bless you all.

Love at First Sight

A candle burns until the flame runs dry. It doesn't flicker on and off or exuberate nasty flames; it just burns at the same brightness until the flame runs dry. That's how I choose to live now. I won't allow anything to falter or affect me anymore, it's safer this way. My name is Kitsu Bolton and I'm 21 years old, I have a small and concise circle of friends but no boyfriend. I built up a wall around my heart many years ago and no one has been brave enough to knock it down ever since.

It all started when I fell in love with a boy at secondary school called Trevor. He wasn't just any ordinary boy – or so I thought – there was something special about Trevor. Something that put a sparkle in my eye and butterflies in my stomach. Trevor wasn't particularly good looking or charming for that matter, but he knew how to carry himself so that all of us girls would just go weak at the knees, the moment he so much as even looked in our direction.

He was a scruffy, rebellious type of boy - everything a young teenage girl could dream of, so I thought! He would always walk around with his shirt untucked, the top button of his school shirt undone, and his winter coat on inside the building at all times. We weren't allowed to wear coloured coats at school, only black ones. Trevor would always wear a navy-blue puffy coat as he strolled down the hallway almost thirty minutes late, every single morning. We knew that Trevor was coming down the corridor because there would always be a yelling and shrieking sound that followed closely behind him. That was Mr Mayhew, the Vice-Principal. Mr Mayhew spent most of his mornings shouting at Trevor about the fact that he was late, or that he was wearing the incorrect uniform once again! The fascinating thing about Trevor was that he didn't seem to care; he would make that known more than anything else he did. Trevor was so uninterested in following the school rules - it was almost as if his refusal to conform made him even more appealing.

"I don't care, I don't care, lock me up for it!" Trevor would repeat with the most sarcastic tone ever uttered as he strutted off down the hallway, with his head bobbing in complete defiance of the Vice Principal's instructions. There was one occasion where Trevor made a massive scene on the ground floor corridor, right outside my classroom. Mr Mayhew was telling Trevor that he was going to be writing a report about his poor behaviour and sending a letter home. We all heard Trevor shouting back at Mr Mayhew.

"Write a report then fam, cool write a report!"

Needless to announce, Trevor spent most of his time sitting in the school's internal exclusion unit.

Despite all of his unfortunate mishaps and outbursts of defiance, there was just something about Trevor that had all of us girls completely lovestruck. Whenever we heard him walking down the hallway, we would try and peer out of our classroom windows to catch his eye. Sometimes we would try and find some kind of excuse to get out of the classroom, so that we could 'accidentally' bump into him in the hallway and steal a cheeky little conversation with him first thing in the morning – well once he finally arrived at school.

I had two best friends at Secondary School called Lisa and Jessica.

Lisa, Jess and I all fancied Trevor although we never really spoke about it openly. I'm not quite sure why we didn't talk about it, but I can only assume it was because secretly, we were all hoping that one day Trevor would ask one of us out and we didn't want it to be awkward for the others. To avoid any future complications, we just chose not to talk about it. Even when we had conversations about the boys at school, none of us really spoke about our real feelings for Trevor. We just kind of skated over it. I remember one time we were having lunch in the school canteen; I caught Jess looking at Trevor from the side of her eye as he walked past. Trevor gave a tiny smirk back. Lisa and I both noticed but we pretended that we didn't. I could tell Jess desperately wanted us to bring it up so she would have some excuse to talk about him, but we didn't.

"He's so ridiculous," we would all snigger whenever Trevor pulled one of his obstinate stunts that landed him back in the Vice Principals' office.

"Yeh, he really needs to get a life," that's what my friend Jess would say.

I remember the first time that I met Trevor, I was in Year 9; I was thirteen years old at the time. Trevor didn't join our school until we were in Year 9, that's the third year of secondary school over here in London – it's what the American's call Junior High. Trevor would've been a Freshman in High School if he had stayed in New Jersey with his mum, that's where he lived for most of his life. Trevor dropped back a school year when he returned to London; he started school mid-year so needed time to catch up on the curriculum. Trevor grew up in London but

3

when he was five years old, his parents split up and he moved to New Jersey with his mother. Trevor lived in New Jersey for about seven years; he moved back to London when he was twelve years old because his mum remarried and moved to the Congo with her new husband. Trevor's dad didn't want him moving to Africa, so he sent for him to come and live with him in London. That's how we met.

Trevor attended a different school, somewhere in North London when he first moved over here; then he transferred to our school in Camberwell as part of a 'managed move.' That's what they call it when you have to move schools because your behaviour is too unmanageable. Although Trevor was placed into our year, he was older than us, only by a year or two though. From the moment Trevor joined our school he had this reputation for being the 'bad guy' in school.

So why would he want to go out with me? I used to sit and wonder as I sat daydreaming about what it would be like to walk hand in hand with Trevor around the hallways of the school. I imagined everyone would be super jealous of me and I could do whatever I wanted. No one would mess with me if I were Trevor's girlfriend, so I thought. He was the boy that everyone looked up to. What would he want with a goody-two-shoes like me though?

There was one day that I walked past Trevor in the hallway, by accident, it wasn't like I planned it or anything; we just ended up being the only ones in the hallway at that particular moment in time. I had walked past Trevor many times before but this one was different – this time Trevor stopped, and he glimpsed at me. It wasn't just any kind of glimpse it was extensive, warm and heartfelt. I looked really nice that day, I had my hair straightened but slicked back in a bun and I had on some dark brown eyeliner that I didn't usually wear because we weren't allowed to wear make-up in school. I just wore it that day because Jess wanted to try out a new look on me, she did that sometimes, brought new make-up and asked me whether she could try it out on me just to see how it looked. I didn't mind. I knew I stood out that day and Trevor noticed it as well. So, when Trevor passed by me in the hallway he just stopped and took an extended look.

He looked at me with silent admiration, I could tell that he was in awe because he didn't say anything. Trevor wanted to tell me how amazing I looked; even though he couldn't get the words out I knew, I just knew.

<u>Tuesday 16th September</u>

Dear Diary,

I have fallen in love! This is it for me I'm telling you this is actually it. There's this boy that just joined our school. His name is Trevor. He's different from the other boys at school. Much cooler, much more mature and independent. The only thing is, I didn't think he was ever going to notice me. Well not in that way. But today everything changed! Today I was in the corridor in between lessons because I had to pick up some photocopying for Miss Emerson. I was secretly hoping to see Trevor because he's always out of lessons wandering around the school and guess what... I did. Not only did I see him but even better – he actually noticed me.

I thought Trevor might stop and say something, but he didn't. He didn't need to though, there was just so much chemistry in the air that words were not even needed.

As he walked away my heart sank into my chest, I didn't breathe until he had finished walking past me. I was so nervous; I hope Trevor didn't notice how nervous I was. How embarrassing! I hope I didn't make it too obvious that I was shaking on the inside.

I can't tell anyone about this, I definitely can't tell Jess and Lisa, they won't be able to handle it. No – I just have to keep this to myself and keep on trying to play it cool.

But the reality has hit me, Trevor actually noticed me. I think Trevor might like me.

Why else would he look at me like that?

Kitsu XoXo

2

The Ice-Cream Parlour

I didn't know what I was going to do after that, I mean Trevor had noticed me but what next? I just felt like Trevor would want to be with someone a bit more high-profile, someone he could bunk school with from time to time and spend whole afternoon's together – you know what I mean? Trevor wasn't just the typical fourteen or fifteen-year-old schoolboy.

Trevor was older than me, it was only a year, maybe two, but it seemed like so much more.

There was another girl that used to be in my class in Year 9 called Candice, when she was going out with an older boy, she would always miss school on Tuesday and Friday afternoon. We all knew what she was doing but no one ever said anything to her. She always pretended to be ill when she couldn't come in, but we knew the truth. I didn't see Candice by the time we got to Year 10, there was a rumour going around that she got pregnant and had to drop out of school and look after the baby, but I don't really know. I imagined Trevor would want someone like that, a bit more daring and spontaneous. He wouldn't want someone boring like me – that's what I concluded.

I had never been excluded from school before, I had a detention one time because I forgot to do my Spanish homework but other than that I pretty much played by the rules. I came to every lesson on time with my full equipment; I wore my whole uniform around school unless I was given permission to take my blazer off and I didn't wear much make-up except for the odd occasion because we weren't allowed to wear make-up in school.

Furthermore, I always came in on time in the mornings because more than anything I didn't want phone calls going home to my mother about lateness.

That brings me on to another topic, my mother; she was so strict on me when I was at Secondary School. Mum threatened that if she ever got a call that I was late to morning registration then she would be dropping me to the school gates first thing in the morning and picking me up again every afternoon.

"You'll not be using your phone after 5 pm either," she added just to seal that last bit of icing on the already luxurious cake.

I couldn't even comprehend the thought of not using my phone after 5 pm, I mean how would I communicate with the outside world? Just the thought of it made me feel like a prisoner behind bars. Furthermore, the last thing I needed was mum driving up to the school gates every morning and afternoon; I would look like a right nerd then. There's no way Trevor would want to go out with a sheltered baby like that. So, I made sure I was at school on time every day.

So, as I was saying, the first time I spoke to Trevor, seemed like a day I would never forget. I was in Year 10 by this point so I must have been fourteen by then. I had seen Trevor around school many times, and he looked at me a few times, but I never really got a chance to speak to him until that one unforgettable day. It was 4.30 pm on a Friday, I was at school late working on an art project and Trevor was at school late because he had an hour's detention for 'refusing to follow instructions.'

I strolled out of the gates with my art portfolio in my hand and my school bag in the other. Lisa and Jess weren't around that afternoon. We would usually wait for one another but on this particular afternoon, I had stayed late making a paper machete sculptor as part of my GCSE art display. And that's when I saw him. That's when my heart melted like a soft pink marshmallow all squished up and ready to eat.

"Hey Kitsu," he said with his usual mischievous smirk.

Trevor could talk to me so confidently now because Lisa and Jess weren't around to get jealous and just make everyone feel uncomfortable. Whenever he used to come and stand with us as a group, Jess would stand right in front of him as if she was his girlfriend. It was so annoying! Well, she wasn't there that time, so we really got a chance to speak and get to know each other; it was a real heart to heart conversation.

"Where you off to?" he enquired with an affectionate disposition that caused my insides to crumble into tiny pieces. My whole throat tightened up and I could barely release the words from my mouth.

"Just making my way home," I finally blurted out. I didn't know where Trevor lived or whether he was going anywhere in my direction as I had never left school at the same time as him before. After that, there was a long and awkward silence as we continued towards the school gates.

"What about you; where are you off to?" Trevor continued making conversation with me as we approached the exit.

I had to say something to soothe the butterflies in my stomach. I couldn't tell what was going on in Trevor's mind as he stared suspiciously into the distance.

"Just on my way home," I answered quietly.

"I wanted to go and get some ice-cream," these words dripped from Trevor's mouth like honey.

I took a deep breath waiting for Trevor to finish his sentence.

I inhaled so much oxygen during that deep breath I barely had room to contain it.

"You want to come with me?" he asked.

And that's where it all began, the first day of the rest of my Secondary School education.

I didn't answer straight away, I wanted to let the proposition linger in the air as my mind began to fill with satisfying thoughts of what it would be like to be Trevor's girlfriend. I didn't have to go out with Trevor that day I could have just gone straight home, but it just seemed like an opportunity too amazing to pass up. I didn't answer straight away as I didn't want to sound too eager, so I paused as if I were in deep thought; I wanted to go out with Trevor, but I didn't want him to know that. I didn't want to seem too keen.

"What's the matter? You got a curfew?" he added with a smirk.

I didn't want to look eager, but I didn't want Trevor to think I was too immature for him either.

"No of course not," I sniggered, "I would love to come," I quickly answered.

A thousand questions raced through my mind at that moment. Was Trevor actually asking me out? Did this mean that he wanted me to be his girlfriend? What would Lisa and Jess say about this? I didn't have time for doubts or negativity, so I put all of those bewildering thoughts to the back of my mind and went on my first date with Trevor.

Trevor took me to a new ice-cream café that had just opened on Walworth Road, it was just around the corner from our school. I got to see a different side of Trevor that day, he wasn't the loud and obnoxious boy that causes havoc around the school; he seemed so intelligent, so thoughtful, so responsible.

As we approached the ice-counter Trevor started fiddling

around in his pocket looking for something, he started patting his pockets in an infuriating manner.

"There it is," he finally blurted out after bringing out a rolled-up £10 note from his pocket.

"So, what you ordering then?"

Trevor asked me whilst looking into my eyes and gesturing towards the counter with his right hand. I was too nervous to think at that moment.

"Whatever you're getting I'll have the same."

I replied in a timid voice, hoping the nervous feeling would just disappear and I would be able to enjoy my ice-cream. Trevor ordered us a bubble gum sundae which I ate reluctantly secretly imagining that it was cookie-dough. I got to know more about Trevor that afternoon, he told me about his life living in New Jersey with his mum. Trevor lived in New Jersey with his mum, stepdad and little sister Tiny. Trevor's mum was a white Irish lady, but she lived in America, Trevor's parents met on a holiday in London. After travelling back and forth for a while and having a long-distance relationship, Trevor's mum eventually decided to settle down in London with his father. They were married for a few years; Trevor was the only child that his parents had together. After a while Trevor's parents started having disagreements, his mum wanted to go back and live in New Jersey, but his dad didn't want that, he wanted to stay in London. Eventually they got divorced; Trevor moved back to America with his mum when he was five years old. After a few years, Trevor's mum remarried and had another child; a daughter called Tina, with her new husband. Trevor never really got along with his stepdad, he didn't say why, and I didn't ask. The final straw came when Trevor's stepdad decided he wanted to move the whole family back to the Congo, where he was from. Trevor's father did not want Trevor moving to the Congo, so he flew him back to London to live with him. Trevor asked me about my family life too. I didn't say much except that it was just myself and my mum living at home together.

Then we spoke about the future. Trevor said that when he finished school, he wanted to be a rich family man and own his own business. He wasn't quite sure exactly what kind of business he wanted to run but he mentioned a rich uncle that lived in West London who was a car manufacturer. Trevor also added that he wanted his wife to be at home looking after the kids whilst he went out and earned money to look after the family. I never really saw myself as a housewife, I wanted to be an Architect and create designs for famous buildings and monuments all over the world. Well, that was until I met Trevor, the thought of being the wife of a rich car manufacturer wasn't something I would have thought of for myself but once Trevor started speaking about it, the whole lifestyle just sounded so appealing.

After our date that afternoon Trevor walked me home. Just as we got to the corner of Camberwell Green, Trevor stopped by the traffic lights, that's where he looked me straight in the eyes and officially asked me to be his girlfriend.

<u>Friday 8th December</u>

Dear Diary,

I've just had the most amazing time! I went out with Trevor after school and I'm still on cloud nine. I think that I just need to pinch myself in order to wake up. I just knocked my foot on my bedpost on purpose to see if it would hurt. It did hurt though! Maybe that wasn't such a good idea. Ouch! I didn't think I would be able to feel any pain right now.

I'm even too excited to sleep. I imagined this moment, but I didn't think it would ever happen. I mean ever!

But now it has actually happened. It has actually, actually happened.

This evening Trevor asked me to be his girlfriend. The way he did it was so sweet, he started speaking to me in a soft, quiet voice. I think Trevor was nervous because I've never heard him speak so quietly before.

Trevor said he likes the way that I smile, and he loves the colour of my hair. He said that he's never seen anyone as unique looking as me and that I'm one of the coolest people he's ever met. I couldn't believe that Trevor actually thought I was cool. Wow, I feel so special.

When Trevor asked me to be his girlfriend you know that I just couldn't wait to say yes, yes, yes!

Kitsu XoXo

Our Secret?

The next day at school I just played it really cool, I mean I was over my nerves and I felt that Trevor had really opened up to me. It was almost like we had formed a proper bond, no need to play games anymore right? I could just be myself around him.

Monday 11ᵗʰ December

Dear Diary,

Trevor called me today for the very first time. I almost didn't want to pick up the phone, I just left it to ring for a while so that I could see his name up on my screen. Then I picked up the phone, but I got nervous, really nervous all of a sudden and I couldn't speak. Seriously this awkwardness just needs to stop.

Kitsu XoXo

Being Trevor's girlfriend wasn't easy at all. It was one of the hardest decisions that I ever had to make. Sounds quite silly now that I think about it but at the time it really was. My whole life had changed and there were so many things for me to consider.

Firstly, telling mum about it was a tricky situation in itself. Mum didn't want me to have a boyfriend at all, she was worried that I might do something silly and then end up pregnant; alone and with no education. Mum always seemed to think the worst in these types of situations, she would always come up with the worst-case scenario she could think of to put me off the idea of even looking at boys.

"Focus on yourself, focus on your education and become the best version of yourself that you can be." That was mum's advice to me.

I remember one-time mum took me out for dinner at Pizza Express in Canary Wharf, it was days before my fifteenth birthday and mum said she just wanted to spend some quality time with me. I could tell she just wanted to know what was going on in my life and whether I had a boyfriend yet. It was so obvious from the way that mum kept smiling and asking me questions.

"So, is there anything new with you?" mum asked in anticipation.

Growing up mum and I used to have these mother-daughter dates once in a while; it was our quality time together. Mum always wanted to know what was going on in my life and most of the time I told her. But then again most of the time it was to do with things going on at school and outings I wanted to go on with my friends. That was fine, I could talk to mum about anything, clothes, friends, my plans for the weekend. It was just that when the topic of boys arose, mum and I didn't really see eye to eye. Mum had already made her thoughts on the matter perfectly clear. I didn't have anything new to share with mum that evening anyway, that was before I started talking to Trevor, so it wasn't like I was hiding anything.

"No mum, just focusing on myself," I reassured her whilst biting into my thinly sliced chicken and mushroom pizza.

"Ok sweetheart, you've got plenty of time for all of that later," mum added.

Then, mum went off into one of her long stories about how young she was when she had me and how difficult things were for her being a single mother. Mum always said that I was one of the best things that happened to her, I didn't feel like I was a burden to her or anything and she never made me feel like I was. I could tell that mum just wanted me to do better, I knew mum had my best interests at heart and she just didn't want me to make the same mistakes that she felt she had made. I guess some lessons are best learned through experiences, even if they are bad ones. Whenever mum spoke to me and gave me her advice about boys, I found myself listening intently and taking everything on board. Oftentimes I would just smile, nod, and go along with what mum told me to do. I wasn't too bothered about having a boyfriend anyway. That was until I met Trevor of course, and that's when I realised that meeting the right person will change your life.

I knew for a fact that Trevor was not the sort of boy that my mother would approve of – not at all. I mean Trevor was older than me and his tough exterior made him seem like a bit of a rebel at times. However, Trevor was just misunderstood, I knew a different side of him. The warm, caring, and thoughtful side – that's who I wanted mum to see when the time was right. So given the circumstances, I did the best thing that I thought I could do, I kept it from her. Well at least for the first few months. That was a major mistake if ever there was one.

Mum and I had always been close, dad left us when I was six years old and it's just been the two of us since then. Mum didn't talk about dad that much and that was fine with me. When she did talk about him it always seemed so negative, it was as if mum kept replaying situations that had happened between the two of them, and when she mentioned his name it all came back to her. Mum said that dad tried to keep her oppressed, she said he never appreciated her and always made her feel like she was worthless. Then she would stop mid-conversation and say, "well that's all in the past now." It didn't feel like it was all in the past because whenever mum spoke to me about the things my father did, she spoke as if these things happened just yesterday. However, she always ended her trip down memory lane by saying, "but that's not your fault sweetheart."

I didn't remember much about my father because I hadn't seen him for almost nine years, I had spent more of my life away from him than I did with him. I always knew that I would recognise him though, if I was to see him in the street, I knew that I would recognise him. My father was a tall man, with long legs and a slim torso. He had a narrow, chiseled chin bordered by a faint black beard. I remember how he used to lift me up and swing me around in the air. I remember us being on a family holiday at a caravan park when I was six years old. When I close my eyes that's where I see my father smiling and swinging me around in the air. I still see mums face peering through the curtains from the inside of the caravan and watching us. Mum didn't come outside to join us that day, I don't know why mum didn't come outside and join us. That's the last memory I have of us being together as a family – mum, dad and I.

I spent the majority of my childhood angry at him. I was angry at him for leaving us and perhaps even more angry at the thought of him coming back. More than anything I just didn't know what I would say to him if he roamed back into our lives again after all of these years. I mean what do you say to a person that walked out and abandoned you as a child? Mum constantly reassured me that my dad didn't leave because of me; that I shouldn't blame myself. It's not that I ever blamed myself, to be honest, I didn't think too much about why he left I just hated the fact that he abandoned us. Just the thought of it made me feel cold and eerie, it sent loose shivers down my spine.

"The day that my father left us," saying it aloud brings back the memory and the pain that goes along with it.

I tried not to talk about him too much, I thought that would make it easier to deal with. Sometimes it's easier to pretend that people never really existed than to remember them and have to deal with the pain of their absence. I remember that day like it was just yesterday, waking up one morning to a teddy bear and a card saying, 'Daddy loves you.' That was the last time I ever heard from my father.

Mum and I didn't speak about him that much after that day either. It was only when I got a bit older, around the age of fourteen that mum started speaking about him again, but that was more from her perspective, how he made her feel as opposed to his ability to be good as a father. I didn't have much to say about my dad because I didn't know him.

As I already had one absent parent in my life, the last thing that I wanted was for my relationship with my mother to be wrecked as well. Especially not over a boy, so despite all of the excitement, the popularity and the butterflies in my stomach, it was a really tough decision for me to become Trevor's girlfriend. When I thought about telling mum about Trevor all I could hear were her warnings ringing about inside of my ears.

"Be careful with these young boys," mum would always tell me, "they will mess you about and leave you broken."

I told myself that mum won't understand; that Trevor was different; he's not like other boys. At this point, I was fifteen years old and I felt ready to make this decision for myself, having to deal with being abandoned by my father and listening to my mother's resentment of him made me feel a lot more mature than other girls my age. I was ready to make a decision like being Trevor's girlfriend. Although Trevor was only two years older than me, I always felt as though he was so much more mature. Everything just seemed so right, but I knew that mum wouldn't understand. I just couldn't imagine a conversation whereby mum would be completely open-minded and understanding about the whole thing. I couldn't imagine her telling me that Trevor was a great guy and that she was happy for me to continue seeing him. I wanted to tell mum about Trevor, but I guess the time never really seemed right.

So, I did what I thought was the best thing I could do all around - I carried on seeing Trevor behind mums back.

<u>Tuesday 24th January</u>

Dear Diary,

It's just so difficult talking to mum, I don't think she'll ever understand. I think she just sees me as a miniature version of her. I feel like she wants to relive her life through me. I can't even tell her about Trevor, not how I really feel about him because she'll just start to panic and tell me to cut off the relationship. She'll probably go from zero to a hundred and start talking about babies and all sorts. It's not even that deep! I just really like Trevor and I like being in his company that's all.

Why do I feel so alone though? I never thought I'd say this but its weird keeping secrets from mum. I guess this is just one of those things that I hoped we could share.

Mum acts like she's never been in love before. It's like she just wants me to stay away from every boy I meet. It's so hard talking to her sometimes we just seem to be on completely different planets. I know it's coming from a good place, but I just wish she'd let me find my own way. I wish she could just be happy for me.

Kitsu xoxo

First Kiss

So, Trevor started off as the perfect gentleman, he didn't rush me into anything that I wasn't ready for, just what I wanted. I told Trevor that I never had a boyfriend before, and that mum didn't want me to have one because she just wanted me to focus on my education. Besides, she was worried that I might do something silly and then end up pregnant and alone-Just another statistic. Trevor looked at me with eyes of understanding, then he said something that I didn't expect him to say.

"I understand, I guess she just wants the best for you," then he smiled at me with the most endearing look. I wanted to cry. I wanted to break down and cry, I so badly wanted mum to meet Trevor for herself. Only then would she understand how wonderful he was. Trevor was so different from any of the other boys in my school. I told Trevor that I just wanted to take things as slowly as possible.

"Yes, so do I," Trevor replied.

I remember one particular night, this was about two months into our relationship, Trevor decided to surprise me. It was a Thursday evening, I was sleeping but I received a message on my phone, it was Trevor telling me that he was standing outside my bedroom window. He said that he missed me and wanted to see me; it was really late at night.

"What are you doing here?" I replied to Trevor's message.

Trevor messaged me back and said that I should come and meet him downstairs. Then I heard a tapping sound on my window glass, it was Trevor throwing tiny pebbles that he must have found on the ground. It was really late, almost 11:30 pm, I don't know what he was thinking he could have woken mum up. I wasn't upset with him though; I thought that it was so romantic. I felt like I was in a modern-day enactment of Romeo and Juliet. Trevor stood on the grass outside on the front lawn, he stood there throwing stones at my window to get my attention. My room is at the front of the house, luckily for Trevor mums' room is at the back so she wasn't awoken by his spontaneous display of affectionate stone-throwing.

I recall that night like it was just yesterday.

Trevor was persistent, finally, I peered outside of my bedroom window after swooping my neatly frilled curtains to one side. Trevor was standing in the moonlit street wearing a ripped denim jacket and jeans; carrying a bunch of violets. My eyes welled up, I felt like I was in the middle of a scene from a love story. I didn't actually know what Trevor wanted me to do at that point or why he had chosen this particular time to come and visit me. I didn't want to come downstairs at first, I was a little bit worried as well. I mean I lived on the outskirts of Peckham, on a dark secluded road right opposite Burgees Park, it's not the type of place you want to go walking around by yourself in the middle of the night. Trevor didn't seem to care though, that's what made him so amazing, he was just so daring and adventurous he would risk his life to come and see me. I couldn't stand there conversing with him from my bedroom window because my mum would've heard me. I would've never been allowed out of my room again! Trevor must have had the same thought because he stopped throwing the pebbles after a while and he moved away from the front of the house. Then he sent me another message to say that I should meet him downstairs on the corner of my road – it wasn't a long walk because I lived just three houses away from the corner of the road.

Senselessly, I jumped into the first pair of jeans that I could grab hold of, put on a nice flowery top pulled my hair up in a messy bun and tiptoed my way downstairs. I peeled open the front door as slowly as I could, frantically endeavouring not to make any noise. Trevor had put his hood up by this point, the closer I got the more I could see his mysterious eyes and mischievous, roguish grin. Part of me was drawn away by the romance in this dangerous gesture whereas the other part looked about circumspectly paranoid that mum would appear right behind me at any minute. I ran to Trevor and swung one arm around his neck and grabbed hold of my flowers with the other. I stood still in the moment thoughtfully deciding where I would hide the flowers in my crowded little first-floor bedroom.

Trevor and I stood for a moment glaring at each other; I just couldn't wipe away the grin that was stretched across my face. I was so unexplainably happy that day.

"Don't I get a kiss then?" Trevor asked. So, I poked my cheek out at him in a cute endearing way.

"I can't believe you're giving me your cheek!" Trevor exclaimed.

I don't know what Trevor was so shaken up about, we never kissed before that day. At this point Trevor and I had only been going out for a month or two, it was still early days. But again, I still didn't want Trevor to think that I was too immature for him. I was so excited about the flowers that he brought me and the fact that he had snuck out of his house to come and see me in the middle of the night. I wanted that moment to last forever.

Standing under a lonesome streetlamp, on an isolated corner of my street next to the rose bush, I swung my arms around Trevor's neck in a burst of excitement. Smirking, Trevor leaned towards me...there it was our first kiss.

We sat on the corner of a brick wall staring into each other's eyes for the better part of five minutes. I had been brave enough creeping out of my house at this time and I didn't want to risk mum coming into my room to find out that I had gone. I gave Trevor a tight hug and then ran back up towards my doorstep. He smiled as he watched me walk away. We didn't say much but we knew something had shifted for us that day. I felt like real love was in the air.

<u>Friday 9th February</u>

Dear Diary

Please don't tell me I just had my first kiss ever! It wasn't just any kiss though; it was with Trevor. I didn't know what to expect, I mean I'd never kissed anyone before. I was worried that I was going to do something wrong, but Trevor just made it seem so easy.

I can't sleep right now, I'm just too excited to sleep. This must be what love feels like because I didn't want that moment to end. Well it had to end because I had to run back home before mum noticed that I was gone. I wish I could share this moment with my mum, lets just keep it between ourselves for now.

Kitsu XoXo

The Secret is Out

The next day at school things felt different. Okay so it was official, there was no going back I was Trevor's official 'grown-up' girlfriend. The next step was to let my mother know that I had met someone – I did have a boyfriend now. Just the thought of speaking to mum about a boy just made my insides cringe all over again. I already knew what she was going to say, and I didn't want to hear it. I knew that I couldn't keep hiding it from her though, it didn't make any sense, mum and I always shared major events in my life, I felt guilty keeping this one to myself. I was sure she had figured it out by herself in any event.

I remember the day that I finally broke the news to mum about Trevor, she was the first person I told. I didn't want Trevor to be there when I told her because I was afraid of how she was going to react. That's why I decided that I was going to speak to her by myself first. It was a Friday afternoon after school and mum was in the kitchen peeling potatoes. I couldn't focus all day at school because I dreaded the conversation that I knew was going to take place that afternoon. By this time Trevor and I had been together for three months, I don't know how we kept it a secret for so long it was eating me up inside. Every time Trevor would walk me back to my house he would stop just around the corner underneath the shelter of the newsagent. We would say our goodbyes there and I would stroll inside my house and run straight up to my room. I figured that if mum saw me straight away, she would know that something wasn't right. But this afternoon was different. Today was a day that a seemingly extraordinary type of boldness and confidence took control of me. I was ready to talk to my mother about my boyfriend. Wow, I can't even believe that I can say this. This was the boyfriend that mum told me not to have. Nevertheless, I had decided that the time was right.

"Hi mum," I uttered nervously as I wandered into the kitchen my heart throbbing so hard, I felt as though it was actually inside my throat. Mum looked at me sternly, I felt like her eyes could see into my soul. It was almost like she already knew what I was going to say, and she had already formed a response. Sweating with anxiety, my palms grew warmer until the warmth turned to a hot and unbearable heat.

"Hi Sweetheart," mum continued in a calm, pleasant tone.

Mum was probably wondering why I had wandered into the kitchen as my usual routine was to head straight for the stairs and into my room. Before I could start running, mum invited me to take a seat at the kitchen table.

"I need to speak to you about something..." mum got in there before I did. The throbbing in my throat had turned into to an excruciating pain, my voice went quiet and breathless, I could hardly speak.

"She knows," I told myself, "she knows everything, it's all over."

That day felt like a déjà vu, all of a sudden, the last three months of my life seemed to flash before my eyes, and I was overcome by an encompassing feeling of panic, grief and loss.

In that moment anxiety came over me, I felt like my lifeline was about to be snatched from the palm of my hands and there was nothing I could do about it. Before my mother uttered her next set of words I burst into tears, uncontrollable and heartfelt tears.

"Please don't stop me from seeing Trevor!" I blurted out in a blubbering mess, at this point I was sobbing uncontrollably, and mum was startled in amazement at the emotional wreckage that sat before her.

"Stop you from seeing Trevor?" mum asked in a voice that sounded both empathetic and uneasy.

That's when I realised that mum had no idea what I was upset about, she didn't have a clue. Well, I had said it and it was too late to retract the statement; with those words, it felt as though a burden of guilt had been lifted from my shoulders. I felt light; I didn't need to keep up the pretence any longer. Mum knew about Trevor, so I didn't have to hide and sneak around anymore. It was such a great relief.

The funny thing is, that wasn't even what mum wanted to talk about, I guess it was just the pressure of keeping secrets from mum that made me break down.

"Your school called!" mum changed the subject abruptly.

"Your punctuality has deteriorated over the past few weeks; you've been arriving late for morning registration every single day."

I kept silent. I had no words for that moment. You know when you wish that you could freeze the frame, go back in time and undo what just happened?

"My school called?" I asked in a half-relieved tone.

But it was too late by then I had already given mum way too much information than was needed for that moment. There was nothing I could do, I just had to continue on and hope for the best.

"That's what you wanted to talk about?" I continued on

with slight hesitation not knowing in which direction this conversation was going to go.

I paused for a moment, my eyes flooded with tears by this point, I had already broken down and told mum everything. Well almost everything, so I waited to see what she was going to say next. Mum handed me a box of tissues to wipe my eyes with, then she looked at me with a longing expression, not saying anything for a while.

"So, who is this Trevor that you're snivelling on about?" Mum began.

I looked down feeling defeated, how could I begin to defend my relationship with Trevor when the very thing my mum was worried about was already showing signs of happening? It was one of those moments where you know your mum is in the right but the worst thing you can do is agree with her. There was just too much at stake. There was no going back, not for Trevor and I, we had fallen so deeply in love that nothing was going to separate us.

"A boy from school mum," I continued.

"He's a really nice guy mum, we've been together for a few months now."

Mum looked at me without saying a word; I could sense the disappointment; it was written all over her face. I knew what she was thinking, she was angry that my school had called her and that my punctuality had slipped but she was even more disheartened that I hadn't been upfront with her from the start. It was like I could hear her thoughts saying, "Three months, three months?"

That was the day that I told mum everything – well almost everything – about Trevor and I.

I told her that afternoon about how much of a gentleman Trevor was, he would always come and meet me around the corner from my house in the mornings and we would walk to school together. I explained to mum that Trevor and I would take the long way to school so that we could stroll through Burgees

Park together and talk. It would have been a lot easier if mum approved of Trevor because then we wouldn't have been sneaking around so much. I guess she figured that out herself because after I confessed everything that had gone on for the past three months, mum responded with something that shocked and amazed me. Of all the responses I could think of that definitely wasn't one of them.

"When are you bringing Trevor round for dinner?" Mum asked with a glaring expression.

I didn't know what to think. I smiled. I stood in awe. I was overwhelmed with delight. I never expected mum to respond like that, but I guess she opted for the lesser of two evils. If she didn't approve of Trevor then I would have had to carry on seeing him behind her back, at least this way everything was kept out in the open. I couldn't wait to tell Trevor that mum knew about him and that she had invited him round for dinner.

Finally, everything seemed to be falling into place.

<u>Saturday 22nd March</u>

Dear Diary,

Now that mum knows about Trevor and I, things are going to be so much better.

I mean I didn't tell mum everything of course - not about Trevor coming around late at night and me sneaking out to meet him. There was no need to tell her about that. Let's just keep that between us. I'm really happy that mum knows about him though, it just makes everything so much easier. I can't wait to see Trevor tomorrow and tell him all about this. I hope he's as excited as I am!

Kitsu xoxo

Ok so I didn't tell mum everything, I just told her what she needed to know. The only time I shared everything was in my diary. I remember the first time that mum read my diary. I was livid, absolutely livid. Mum said that she was clearing up my room and had just "stumbled" across it. I think that I may have left it open on my bedroom cabinet, but that's not the point anyway. The point is that mum should have respected my privacy. She read the part where I divulged all of my deepest, heartfelt feelings for Trevor. So embarrassing! I didn't speak to mum for weeks after that, not properly. Mum would even say that it was a whole month – who knows? I couldn't even look her straight in the eye for a while, there are some things a girl just wants to keep to herself. Some things should just be kept between the pen and the page. Well, I guess the important thing was that mum knew about Trevor, so we didn't have to sneak around anymore.

Cat Fight

Now that the hard part was out of the way, next on my agenda was to share the news with everyone at school. Unfortunately, Lisa and Jess didn't take the news of me being Trevor's girlfriend so well. Trevor and I had kept our relationship really low key around school. We would hang out in groups and sit near each other whenever we could, but we wouldn't do obvious things like hold hands or sit down and have lunch together where it was just the two of us. Trevor said that he didn't want everyone knowing our business, at least not right at the beginning of things. It was quite fun having a secret relationship with Trevor, but once mum knew about it there didn't seem to be much point in keeping it a secret anymore.

So, the following week at school we decided to make the official announcement. I started by telling Lisa and Jess. It was lunchtime and we were all sitting around the wooden benches outside. Trevor walked past us as he usually does, he smiled and winked at me then went across to the fields to play football with his friends. So that's the day that I decided to break the news to them.

"I've got something to tell you," I started in a soft, peaceful tone.

I felt like I was breaking terrible news about some major life-changing event. It shouldn't have felt that way, they were my best friends, after all, there was no real reason why they couldn't just be happy for Trevor and I. Jess and Lisa went quiet and bent their ears towards me in anticipation of what I was about to say.

"What is it?" Jess asked with an eager but slightly hesitant disposition.

They had no idea that the news I was about to break could determine the course of our whole friendship, I knew they both fancied Trevor, so it was a make or break moment for us. Would they still want to be my friends once they knew that I was the one that Trevor really wanted? Could they be happy for Trevor and I? I couldn't answer either way with confidence. So, I eased them in slowly, watching and studying to see how they reacted to each bit of information as it came.

"I've been seeing someone." I began as they both gasped in amazement.

"Who...is it someone from school?" Lisa enquired in an excited voice.

"Well yes actually, it is someone from school," I smiled.

"Who is it?" Lisa and Jess asked at the same time both leaning in towards me eyes wide open.

"Well, it's Trevor actually," I blurted out with a girlish grin spread right across my face.

"I've been seeing Trevor for the past few months, but we made it official not too long ago."

They both paused without speaking so I looked at them and continued.

"I told mum about him last week as well and she can't wait to meet him."

There was an extremely awkward silence, then Lisa started to snigger.

"What's so funny?" I asked whilst assuming that she was just jealous.

"You're not going out with Trevor?" Lisa blurted out in disbelief. At that point, I started to feel a little insulted.

Why would she assume that I had made this all up? I pondered to myself for a moment.

Jess didn't say anything, she just listened to Lisa rattle on about how I was delusional and that she felt I must be making all of this up because Trevor supposedly liked her and not me. I couldn't believe what I was hearing. I knew that we all secretly liked Trevor at one point, but I didn't expect it to get to a point where we could no longer be friends because he chose one of us. I didn't want Trevor to hear this conversation either, it was so embarrassing. I knew why Jess kept silent, she wanted to be Trevor's girlfriend too. I think I preferred that response rather than the insults and cattiness that I was getting from Lisa.

Lisa kept going on and on about the same thing, she was insisting that I had gotten the wrong impression and that Trevor was just trying to be nice to me.

"Nah, you're got the wrong end of the stick babe," she spoke in an obnoxious, patronising manner, whilst waving her hands around in all different directions.

"I don't believe that for a moment," Lisa added.

I felt slightly insulted. I mean, what was so hard to believe? In that moment, whilst Lisa was rambling on, I didn't know how much more I could take; I felt like a deep, fire had ransacked my insides. Eventually, I burst, I couldn't contain it, so I shouted at Lisa and told her to "shut up!" I also told her that she was, "Just jealous of our relationship."

That's when Lisa did something completely outrageous; something that I never expected in a million years, she jumped and attacked me and started pulling at my hair with both of her hands. She was shouting and screaming about how I was such a terrible friend and that I had supposedly stolen her boyfriend. Embarrassing! Absolutely embarrassing! Of course, I had to defend myself, so I started pulling at her hair and scratching at her face to get her off of me. We both ended up in a grappling match in the middle of the outdoor seating area of the school courtyard. Seriously, I couldn't believe what was happening, Lisa and I had never gotten into a physical fight before, I couldn't believe what was happening. It happened so quickly. She provoked me and I snapped.

What was even more strange is that Jess was desperately trying to pull us apart whilst telling Lisa to, "Let me have him."

"Let me have him?" I looked at Jess out of the side of my eye half-questioning her motives and intentions by this point. Was she trying to break up the fight or was she just using this as a way to vent out her frustrations?

How was Jess telling Lisa to let me have him? He was already mine. I had never heard anything so ridiculous in all of my days; I mean I didn't realise that someone could take jealousy to such extreme levels.

The fight continued until the teachers on playground duty came and broke it up. By this time half of the school were crowded around us and causing a huge uproar shouting "FIGHT, FIGHT, FIGHT!" We both ended up in the Head Teachers office that day; needless to say, we got externally excluded - for two whole days.

<u>Thursday 6th April</u>

Dear Diary,

I'm so angry right now. I cried so much today, I cried to release my anger, but it didn't work. I can't believe I got excluded for fighting with one of my best friends. I mean I didn't want to fight with her, but I had to defend myself. What was I meant to do? Now everything is just a mess because mum knows that I got into a fight. Well, she doesn't know that it was over Trevor though. Let's just keep that part between us. Shhhh!

I never thought that something like this would happen, not to me. These are things you read about in magazines and see in the movies. You just never expect it to be your own life!

I mean I know that we all secretly liked Trevor, but I guess I just hoped that one day when Trevor finally did express his true love for me... well ... I guess I just hoped that my friends would be happy for me. I can't believe they both switched on me like that, wow over a boy that was never even theirs. I guess we weren't friends after all then.

I'm not going to lie, it is going to be really difficult not having Lisa and Jess in my life, especially at school, but at least I have Trevor.

I guess Trevor is everything to me now.

Kitsu xoxo

He's Controlling

I didn't speak to Lisa and Jess much after that fight, our friendship pretty much deteriorated. I would see them around the school, but we couldn't connect like how we used to due to all of the jealousy.

I remember the day I came back from my exclusion, I know everyone was talking about me and I felt like such a rebel in school. I could tell Trevor was impressed as well, finally; I did something that was out of the norm. It was like I was slowly moulding into the type of girl that Trevor always wanted. No longer the goody two shoes that he once thought I was. That afternoon, Trevor walked me home as usual but this time we did it openly. With confidence, we walked out of the school gates hand in hand and everyone knew that I was Trevor's girlfriend. It was official for all the world to see; I was so chuffed. Nothing else mattered to me whilst I was with Trevor.

I spent most of my time with Trevor after that, in school and outside as well, he came around to my house to meet mum as well. When Trevor met mum, he was the perfect gentleman, just like he was on our first date at the ice-cream parlour.

"Afternoon mum," Trevor being his usual confident and cheeky self, greeted mum with the warmest of tones.

I waited in expectation, I really wanted mum to like Trevor, I wanted her to see the kind, generous and loving side of him, just like I did. That evening, we sat down at the dining table - Trevor, mum and I. Mum and I rarely actually ate at the dining table, since it was usually just the two of us, we just kind of held onto our plates and sat down in the front room. I could tell that Mum wanted to make a special effort for Trevor; she wanted to make him feel welcome in our home. I was grateful because it showed me that mum trusted me, and she wanted me to be happy. Throughout dinner I kept on glancing at mum to see her reaction every time that Trevor spoke. Mum didn't give much away, but it wasn't as tense and uncomfortable as I imagined it would be. I still don't think that mum approved of Trevor, not really but I was pleased that she had accepted him even if it was just for my benefit. I was on top of the world, cloud nine even; I felt as though nothing could go wrong. Little did I know, I was poised unsuspectingly at the top of a downwards spiral.

Five months into our relationship things took a turn for the worse, Trevor started to become very distant after we had our first major argument, it didn't even seem like a big issue. I thought we would have gotten over it by the next day, but we didn't.

<u>Saturday 7th May</u>

Dear Diary,

I've been looking at my phone all day expecting Trevor to message me. He hasn't. Was it really that much of a big deal? I don't understand why Trevor has gone cold on me all of a sudden. Was it something I did? Something I said?

You know what, I'm not even going to take this thing too seriously – whatever, it's bedtime now. I'm sure Trevor will call me or something tomorrow.

Kitsu xoxo

It was such a silly argument now that I think about it. It was all because Trevor didn't like me wearing make-up unless I was out with him. He said that I was 'drawing attention to myself' and causing other boys to look at me. I had no idea what Trevor was worried about or why he was acting so paranoid and insecure all of a sudden. Trevor knew that I didn't have eyes for anyone but him. I didn't understand why he was making such a big deal about the whole situation of me wearing some make-up. I never told Trevor what to do or how to dress; there were loads of girls that liked him in our school, but I still didn't tell him what to do about it – I trusted him.

I didn't wear that much make-up before Trevor and I got together, Trevor said he liked the natural look. He said he loved the shape of my eyes because they were almond-shaped but still sharp and pointy in the corners, like a kitten. That's where I got the nickname Kitsu – because of the shape of my eyes.

Trevor also said that he liked my eyelashes because they were naturally long and curled so I didn't need to wear mascara either. There were a few other features of mine that Trevor always commented on such as my hair and the shape of my waist. But once Trevor stopped telling me how beautiful I was and how much he loved my physical features I felt like I had to do more to capture his attention again. It became addictive. Whenever I would see Trevor and he didn't compliment me, I would start to feel low about myself. If Trevor didn't comment on my hair, then I felt as though my hair was a mess and I had to change it up – so I dyed it. If Trevor didn't tell me how beautiful I looked I felt like he had gotten bored of looking at me. So, bit by bit I started to wear more and more make-up. I didn't want to plaster my face like the girls in the magazines; I didn't want to look like a clown or anything; I just wanted to accentuate the features that I already had. I wanted to keep Trevor interested but for some reason, he thought I was doing it to get attention from other boys. I wasn't doing that, all of Trevor's female friends wore make-up so I thought that it was just the best way to keep him interested, it made me feel more confident in myself as well.

As time went by, I started wearing more and more makeup when I was around Trevor. It started with some extra mascara and eyeliner then eventually I got into wearing foundation and using contour and sometimes even lipstick. I mainly wore the make-up when Trevor and I went out for dates, I just wanted to look my best at all times, and I didn't want Trevor looking at other girls. One time I went out with Trevor and I saw that his eyes had started to wander, another girl walked past us, she wasn't all that pretty, but she was heavily made up and I noticed Trevor looking at her. I didn't ask him about it, but I saw and I knew that it was time for me to step up my game. I couldn't get away with wearing much make-up during school time though. I tried to keep my school make-up subtle so that teachers wouldn't notice it. By the time we got to Year 11 – our final year of Secondary School - the school had enforced this new strict policy on make-up, if we got caught wearing make-up we would have to go straight to the school admin office and remove it with baby wipes or spend the day inside the internal exclusion unit. I couldn't stand the internal exclusion unit, especially because it meant I was separated from Trevor for the whole day.

Anyways, when I first started wearing more make-up Trevor was fine with it. In fact, I could tell that he was really impressed by it. Eventually, in a moment that seemed to come out of nowhere, Trevor just started complaining about everything.

"Why are your cheeks all red?" that's what Trevor would say when he wanted me to take off my blusher.

"I can see my reflection in your forehead," that's what Trevor would say when he wanted to comment on my bronzer.

I didn't understand the reasoning behind Trevor trying to stop me from wearing make-up. I considered his opinion, I really did, but then there was another part of me that just really liked wearing make-up. Not even for Trevor, but just for myself, I got attached to it and it became like my identity.

So, when Trevor told me to stop wearing make-up I did what I had to do - I didn't listen to him! Another major argument started because I told Trevor to stop telling me what to do and to stop speaking to me like he was some sort of dad.

"I don't have time for these petty arguments."

That's what I said to Trevor when I got really angry. I was tired of him bossing me around all of the time, telling me what to do, he was worse than my mum. Trevor didn't like that one single bit, he said that the way that I spoke to him was disrespectful, so he started distancing himself from me and acting really cold. Trevor knew that I would feel lonely during those moments, he knew that I had fallen out with my two best friends over him, but he didn't care. When Trevor stopped talking to me, I experienced some of the lowest moments of our relationship. I couldn't concentrate on anything when Trevor went into one of those sulky moods. It was just so passive-aggressive and made me feel lonely. I knew what Trevor was doing, even back then I knew exactly what Trevor was doing and I hated the way it made me feel.

Trevor started taking hours, sometimes even days to respond to my messages; then when I saw him at school, he would walk past me without saying anything at all. He was cold. Arctic - cold at times.

<u>Friday 2nd June</u>

Dear Diary,

I'm sitting here with tears dropping on to the pages of my diary, someone wake me up from this nightmare!

I've just had my second major argument with Trevor and now he's not even speaking to me. I feel so alone without Trevor by my side I feel empty and shrivelled up on the inside. I haven't heard from Trevor in about two days now. I mean I've been checking my phone every couple of hours in the hope that I will hear something from him; he hasn't said anything at all.

I hate this feeling; this must be what heartbreak feels like and if it is, I don't want it. I don't want to feel like this anymore. I don't know how much more of this I can take.

I can't even tell mum about this... can I? I mean she's trusted me to get on with things now and I just don't want her worrying unnecessarily.

Trevor doesn't like me wearing make-up, so I guess I just won't wear it. I guess he's just looking out for me, right? I suppose this is all for the best. I guess...

Kitsu xoxo

I couldn't stand it when Trevor was distant. I felt like a fish out of water. I didn't know what else to do, so eventually I just succumbed to my emotions and did what Trevor wanted me to do just to keep the peace.

Losing Myself

I wasn't happy living like that. I didn't know how long I could keep up the pretence. Outwardly, I was the girl that everyone wanted to be, Trevor's girlfriend, but inside I was just an emotional wreck searching for completion where I couldn't find it. Suffocated. Restricted. Desolate. It was like I was screaming from the top of my lungs, but no sounds were coming out. Following Trevor around and doing all that he wanted me to do was never going to bring me satisfaction. Deep down I must have known this – I don't know why I kept trying to convince myself otherwise.

Well looking back now I guess I had just gotten so used to the 'wonderful' life that Trevor and I had built up together I couldn't imagine it any other way. I had given up so much for Trevor - friends, family, my good reputation at school. I never got in trouble at school until I met Trevor. He made everything around me change, we had come too far to go back to how things were when we first met. We were in too deep. Even in the difficult times, I felt like it had gotten to a point where I couldn't even imagine life without him.

Unable to eat, sleep or focus on anything, I became an emotional wreck without Trevor by my side. Inevitably my grades started to deteriorate as I was no longer the smart and focused student I once was. My life became consumed by this boy. He was all I could think about most mornings. Waking up checking my phone hoping that Trevor had messaged me whilst I was sleeping; it was both painful and pitiful at the same time. What had my life become?

Thursday 7th July

Dear Diary,

This must be what love feels like. When you need someone in your life to help you take your next breath! When someone messages you just to check up on you and you know just how much they care. Sometimes I scroll through Trevor's old messages on my phone and I just sit there and smile to myself. This must be love.

I didn't see Trevor at school today, but he said that he saw me though. Trevor's always looking out for me at school, I feel like he just wants to know where I am at all times. Yep, I'm convinced, what Trevor and I have is real love.

There's not a day that goes by when I don't think about Trevor and I know that he feels the same way about me. Wow. Love is a good thing. It's such a good thing! If I'm dreaming, then don't wake me up because I just want to stay right where I am.

Kitsu xoxo

If anyone told me this would be my life, I would have denied it vigorously. Seriously, I would have argued against it with my dying breath. These are the things you read about in magazines. I never thought that I myself would one day become that lovesick teenage girl that couldn't function without her boyfriend by her side. But low and behold, slowly but unexpectedly it crept up on me.

I remember every weekday morning, standing in the mirror unable to comprehend what my life had become I let my self slip away, every trace of independence and personal identity. I began to measure myself according to Trevor's standards, instead of my own.

I could hear my mother's voice in my ears telling me, "You're better than this," but I blocked it out ruthlessly. I dressed exactly how Trevor wanted me to dress and I didn't change my hair because Trevor said he liked the subtle, simple look. I wanted to get some light brown highlights to change things up a bit, but Trevor said that it was too extravagant, he just wanted me to blend in and 'be myself.'

There was one particular Saturday that Trevor came to pick me up so that we could go for a walk in the park. I wasn't prepared so I came downstairs to speak to Trevor just to let him know that I needed some time to get dressed. Trevor started complaining about me making him wait downstairs whenever he comes to pick me up, so that's why I started coming down to meet him. That afternoon, I was wearing creased, faded, black trousers, a long blue t-shirt and my hair was flung up in a messy bun. I had a flowery scarf wrapped around my head and I wasn't wearing any make-up at all. This was my 'stay at home no one needs to see me today' type of look.

"You scrub up nicely," Trevor proclaimed. I looked at him wondering whether he was being genuine or sarcastic. I mean I looked like a complete mess.

"I look a mess, Trevor, I've barely even fixed my hair," I replied and I was not fishing for compliments.

"If you never change your hair again – I'm good," Trevor replied looking contended with himself.

Trevor was dressed up. He was wearing a fitted grey Nike tracksuit, with his trousers sagging far below his waistline and some fresh white Air Forces. He looked comfortable and put together. I looked at Trevor for a moment when he reached his hand out towards me so that we could go. I hesitated but I listened to him, grudgingly I listened to him.

At the time it sounded like an outward display of acceptance, almost like Trevor telling me that I didn't always need to make an effort to look good when I was out with him.

Saturday 9ᵗʰ July

Dear Diary,

Today I looked so rough! Trevor came to meet me so that we could go for a walk together. I wanted to go upstairs and change but Trevor didn't want me to. It's not a big deal though is it? I mean clothes aren't everything – I guess Trevor just wants me to know that he loves me just the way I am.

Kitsu xoxo

But now I see things differently. Trevor didn't want me to feel good about myself; he didn't want me to look beautiful, blossom and grow. He just wanted to keep me underneath his control. Trevor didn't mind me going out looking like a mess because at least that way he could be sure that no other guys would look at me, that was his main concern. He was trying to squash me down, slowly and surely. I'm convinced that Trevor just wanted to squash me down bit by bit so that I could crawl into a hole; then come out and start following him around like some dummy. Trevor wasn't confident, he was insecure, he wanted to keep me underneath his thumb. He wanted me in a place where it was comfortable for him, a place where he was on top and I could be kept down. Trevor didn't care about me; it was all about him and eventually I started to see that for myself.

Date Night

There was one particular day that Trevor came to pick me up for a date, he said that we were going to the cinema with a group of his friends from his local area and their girlfriends. Trevor lived about half an hour away from me by car; he lived in Brixton. That evening I was so excited to be going out with Trevor and his friends. I put on the cutest little tracksuit with matching Adidas boots; finishing off the look with a new leather jacket that I got from Camden Market. I decided that I would go for a cute and casual look that night. Trevor came to my door and looked me up and down in disgust.

"Why are you dressed like that?" He grunted as if in horror.

"Like what?" I asked with a disheartened voice.

"I've come to pick you up for a date and you come out here dressed like a boxer!"

"Boxer?" I repeated.

I couldn't believe what Trevor was saying, he just started yelling and insulting me right there on my doorstep. Just the other day Trevor was showing me that it didn't matter what I wore. Then the next week he comes and insults my outfit in the most belittling way. I was so distraught. I wanted to cry but my mascara wasn't waterproof, so I didn't. I spent ages picking out that outfit. I didn't even know how to respond to Trevor's outbursts. I wanted Trevor to approve of how I looked but it seemed that whenever I would adapt my dress style to suit him; he would think of something else to complain about.

Trevor stood on my doorstep, not allowing me to leave the house. He started complaining about my outfit in all kinds of humiliating ways. Trevor started telling me that I looked like a little girl trying to play dress up. I felt so degraded. He told me to go and make more of an effort. I walked back inside my house and went back upstairs to my room. I didn't want to go outside anymore; I didn't want to go to the cinema, and I didn't want to meet Trevor's friends. I imagined myself slamming the door in Trevor's face and leaving him on the doorstep - but then I caught myself. I knew that if I did that then Trevor would get angry and start ignoring me all over again. So, I did the best thing that I could -I went upstairs and changed my outfit. I put on a ripped pair of jeans, a sparkly cropped top and some killer heels. I figured Trevor just wanted to make a good impression. He just wanted to show me off to his friends.

At this point in our relationship, I was fifteen years old; Trevor had just turned seventeen. Trevor's friends were a mixture of seventeen and eighteen years old, but they seemed so much older than us.

After the whole outfit ordeal ended, Trevor and I managed to have a good time at the cinema. Although we were out with a group of his friends, Trevor and I sat on a row of chairs by ourselves. Trevor became the perfect gentlemen once again, he paid for my ticket and asked me if I wanted anything to eat from the food kiosk. I felt so special being out with Trevor.

Mum never used to buy food when she took me to the cinema as a young child, she said it was over-priced and a waste of money. Trevor didn't care about stuff like that, whenever we went out, he would treat me like a princess – at least that's how I felt at the time. So, we ate our food and watched the film. I can't remember what we watched that day – I think it was a Batman movie. I didn't like action movies until I started going out with Trevor, it was something else that he got me into.

We sat alone and watched the film to the end. Once the film had ended everyone got up to leave the cinema, but Trevor and I just stayed in our seats.

"What did you think of the film?" Trevor asked as he was facing towards me.

"It was great I enjoyed it," I replied, looking around at the almost empty cinema.

At this point Trevor was leaning in towards me staring deep into my eyes, that was Trevor's way of asking me for a kiss. I did feel a bit uncomfortable sitting down waiting for everyone to leave the cinema, just so that we could kiss each other. Trevor didn't seem to care though. So, we kissed briefly and then stopped because we realised, we weren't alone.

There were these two ladies that had been sitting on the row behind us, they were still in the screen room discussing what they thought about the film. When Trevor and I started getting close to one another I could feel them both looking at us, whispering and scrunching up their faces. I could feel their eyes piercing into the back of my head. Their looks felt worse than my mothers. It's almost as if they could tell that Trevor and I were just waiting for the cinema to be empty so that we could have some alone time. They must have thought that we were some tacky, hormonal teenagers. I could hear them talking about us. Trevor heard it too, but we acted like we were just talking about the film; we waited for them to leave. There was an awkward silence during their conversation, then they started walking towards the exit. I could hear them murmuring as they walked off.

"What are those two doing?" the first one said.

"You can tell they're just waiting for everyone to leave the cinema," the other lady added.

"How tacky!"

"Don't they have anywhere to go?"

The two ladies continued to natter between themselves as they headed towards the exit door.

Trevor and I must have looked really 'tacky' sitting in an empty cinema after the film had ended just so that we could spend some time alone together. I thought I was so special back then.

<u>Friday 3ˢᵗ July</u>

Dear Diary,

I had the best time with Trevor tonight it was so romantic.

We went to the cinema and we had such an amazing evening. I can tell that Trevor likes me because he paid for my ticket and he brought me cinema food. I always hear women talking about when a man spends money on you then you know that his feelings are real. Trevor spent so much money at the cinema we had sweets, popcorn and ice-cream.

The best part of all is, after the film ended Trevor wanted us to wait in our seats so that we could be alone in the cinema. Then he leaned in and kissed me, this time for much longer than usual.

I've just had the best night ever.

Kitsu xoxo

When I think about it now, we probably did look tacky – I don't know what I was getting so excited about. I can buy my own popcorn in the cinema.

House Party

Trevor and I spent a lot of time together that summer. The following evening, we went bowling with a group of Trevor's friends again; afterwards, one of Trevor's friends, called Chris, invited everyone around to his house for a gathering. By this time mum had pretty much left Trevor and I to get on with our relationship. Her only rule was that I must not be home any later than 10 pm – that was my weekend curfew. Weekdays it was 7 pm. I stuck to it most times! During the summer holidays, mum said that I could just stick with my weekend curfew.

On this particular day, we finished at the bowling alley just after 9 pm; I had just enough time to get home without mum complaining. I should have gone straight home that day, I should have stood my ground, but I didn't. Trevor wanted to go to the after-party at Chris' house. He knew that I had to be home by 10 pm but I guess he didn't want his friends to think that his girlfriend was a complete loser. I was naïve and too afraid to speak up for myself.

"You know that I have to be home by 10 pm," I reminded Trevor subtly.

He gave me a look as if to say, "So what?"

Trevor took me by the hand, and we followed the crowd to Chris' house.

Chris lived in a posh area of London; in a large, detached house; on the corner of a quiet, secluded road. Chris lived in West Dulwich. His parents were away on holiday, so he was home alone for the weekend. Chris' parents were affluent, his basement was the size of the whole first floor of my house. When we got inside, he had bottles of beer laid out neatly along the kitchen counter, also, he had a spread of unopened packets of crisps, biscuits and honey roasted peanuts.

"Help yourself," Chris insisted whilst being the perfect host.

I felt awkward and uncomfortable the moment I entered the room, don't ask me why I stayed but I did. Trevor seemed to be in his element, he put his arm around me like I was his property and led me into the dark, smoky basement. Trevor knew that I felt uncomfortable, but he chose not to acknowledge it. I told myself that he just wanted to make a great impression on his friends. I guess it was just another red flag that I chose to ignore.

It was 10 pm and we still hadn't left the party, I was worried that mum would be sending out a search warrant, but Trevor assured me that everything was going to be fine.

"We'll leave in a minute," he said standing close to my side like a bodyguard.

As more and more people started to arrive, they brought varieties of interesting artefacts with them to the party. By artefacts I mean bottles of gin, vodka, beer cans and roll-ups. I stood next to Trevor silently surveying the disarray that surrounded me.

I loved being with Trevor, but I didn't feel comfortable in that environment with his friends. I didn't want to drink gin; I didn't want to smoke weed, and I didn't want to be in that house.

All I could think about was what mum would say if she knew where I was. She would've been so disappointed.

"Can we go now please?" I wanted Trevor to know that I wasn't comfortable.

"Go where? We just got here!" Trevor exclaimed as if in complete oblivion.

It was obvious that Trevor didn't care how I felt. He was happy, he was in his element.

I just sighed and looked down at my watch wondering when all of this was going to be over. Trevor was completely ecstatic.

"Come on let me introduce you to some people," he continued taking me by the hand and guiding me through the basement.

A whirlwind of mist stirred through the garden as a group of Chris' friends were rolling up tobacco and other herbs so that they could smoke. I didn't want to go into the garden, but Trevor took me there as part of his guided tour of the house. Trevor's friends were passing this rolled up substance around taking one puff at a time.

Standing there hoping that they would know not to pass it to me, something dreadful happened. I blinked and found myself holding this rolled up substance in one hand, Trevor looking at me with eyes of anticipation. What was I going to do next? I stood there for a moment looking at the marijuana rolled up in my hand, then I looked at Trevor.

"Don't just stand there," that's what the girl next to me said.

'Take a puff and pass it around," shrieked another irritating voice.

I was holding up the flow and everyone was looking at me, it felt like hours had gone by in the space of time that they were looking at me with glaring eyes. Trevor didn't say anything he stood next to me and waited for me to make a decision. So, I did.

Curiosity came over me, I wanted to know what was so

fascinating, so I caved in to the peer pressure; I put the substance to my mouth and took a puff. I didn't breathe it in completely because I felt like I was choking, I inhaled it into my mouth and then coughed and coughed and coughed it back out again feeling like my insides were on fire.

At that moment one of Chris' obnoxious friends looked at me and said, "if you don't know how to smoke then don't smoke!"

She was talking like it was an artistic skill such as playing an instrument or crafting the Mona Lisa. I didn't want to smoke anyway, and I was ready to go home. After I finished coughing, I passed the roll up to the next person and I left the circle.

That's when I told Trevor that I wanted to go home and this time I was dead serious. After I left the garden I went straight towards the front door and stood outside.

Trevor followed me.

"You ready to go?" he asked, although already aware of my answer.

Finally, Trevor was showing consideration for my feelings, only took for me to start almost coughing my lungs out.

I didn't answer with words, I just looked at Trevor and nodded. Trevor put his arm around me and gave me a tight hug.

"I need to speak to you in private," he continued.

Looking at my watch and glancing up at Trevor I asked if we could talk about this on the way home – it was getting late; way past my curfew. Trevor looked at me with the boyish grin that I couldn't resist.

By this time, I was shivering as I had left my coat at home that day. I wasn't expecting to be out so late. Trevor offered me his coat, but he said that he had left it inside the house when he came out after me.

"You can't be outside like this babe, let me go in and get you my coat." It was Trevor's protective side that made me feel all weak at the knees and soft on the inside again.

My heart went squishy like a soft pink marshmallow. Trevor's kind gestures could make me forget myself and do almost anything he wanted.

"I want to talk to you before we go, let's talk inside where it's warm."

Trevor led me upstairs to an empty room, it was the guest bedroom, but it looked neatly swept clean and almost unlived in. He sat me down in the corner of a brownish, golden sofa full of cushions and looked intently into my eyes.

"What is all of this about?" I enquired nervously.

"I just want to talk to you," Trevor replied moving close to me and holding me around the waist.

I broke away from Trevor's light grip and folded my arms in frustration whilst looking through the window and into the garden. It's not that I didn't enjoy spending time with Trevor, it's just that it was late.

It was 11 pm and Trevor smelt like vodka. It was hardly the time and place to have a deep heart to heart conversation about the future of our relationship.

That's when Trevor started talking about taking things to the next level. I knew where all of this was going but I felt awkward and uneasy with every word that was uttered from Trevor's mouth. This was the first time that Trevor decided to talk to me about 'taking things to the next level.'

OK, I know what you're thinking, the first kiss was on the street corner, then we're waiting in an empty cinema, now we're sitting in the guest room of a friend's house talking about taking things to the next level. Classy right? Trevor sure knew how to make a girl feel special.

That evening could definitely go down as one of the most awkward nights of our relationship to date. I still don't know why Trevor chose to have that conversation at the end of a house party, smelling of vodka and way past my curfew. Then again, there are a lot of things about Trevor that I still don't understand.

"So, we've been together for ages now," Trevor began.

I quickly interrupted, "it's only been a few months, it's not that long."

I knew where this conversation was going so I wanted to close it down quickly, I always used to hear stories about girls getting pressurised into sleeping with their boyfriends and it always ended in a bad way. It was either the boy would lose interest in the relationship soon afterwards or the girl would just end up pregnant and leave school. Either way, I didn't want that to be me.

Holding hands and going out to the cinema was one thing, the kissing was fine, but I definitely wasn't ready for any 'next level' that Trevor was suggesting. I was only fifteen after all. Mum had warned me about this moment, this is why she was so against me having a boyfriend.

"Just focus on your schoolwork," that's what she would say.

My palms began to sweat, my throat tightened, and I could feel my voice quieting. I just wanted the conversation to end. I just wanted Trevor to stop talking because deep down I knew that if he carried on talking about this, I was eventually going to cave in.

Anxious. Nervous. Panicky. I was boxed into this unavoidable and awkward moment that I knew was going to come sooner or later.

Trevor and I sat in that guest bedroom for the better part of an hour discussing the future of our relationship and where we thought it was going. Trevor said that he wanted to marry me one day, I wasn't even thinking that far ahead but once he said it, I became consumed with blissful thoughts of our enlightening future together. But I didn't want to go to any 'next level' with him. My mother frightened the thought out of me, there was nothing I wanted less than to end up pregnant and alone at just fifteen.

"I don't think I'm ready yet," that's what I told Trevor.

He didn't say much at first, he just looked at me and I could tell he was disappointed. The look of disappointment on Trevor's face hurt more than words could. I felt even worse when Trevor responded with such kindness. I expected him to get annoyed like he did about the clothes and the make-up, but this time he didn't. His response was a bit off.

"No worries, I'll be alright." That's what Trevor said. I didn't know what he meant by that though.

When we went back downstairs after the talk, a room full of eyes were focused on us. The girls were giggling, and the boys were cheering and giving Trevor the nudge and the wink. I felt like I was being judged and criticised by every piercing grin.

I heard Trevor tell them that, "Nothing happened," but the tone in which he spoke sounded disappointed and disheartened again. I became paranoid, I wondered whether Trevor had been boasting about me with his friends and telling them personal things about our relationship. But I didn't say anything about it. We left Chris' house slightly after that conversation and I went home.

<u>Thursday 29th August</u>

Dear Diary

Ok so I've been with Trevor for 8 months now and I think he's getting bored of the relationship. Last night Trevor told me that he wanted us to take things to the next level. I told him that I'm not ready. He seemed to be understanding but I'm not sure if I believe him.

Trevor said that he was going to be ok.

I think that means he is going to go off with someone else. I don't know what to do. I'm only fifteen years old, I'm still so young for all of this. I sound like my mum. I guess it wouldn't be a terrible thing to do – taking things further with Trevor. He is my boyfriend after all. I'm sure all of Trevor's friends' girlfriends have done the same. I can never talk to mum about this, I know what she's going to say.

I need to think about this and make a quick decision. If I don't do something soon then Trevor will probably leave me for someone older and more mature!

What do I do?

Kitsu xoxo

School Calls Mum

That was the last week of the summer holidays, then we went back to school. The next week at school I ended up telling my friend April about what happened at the party. April was lovely. She was in the sixth form. She was three years older than me. April was stunning. She was tall and slender. She had long, dark hair, beautiful brown eyes and a caramel-toned complexion. I wanted to be just like her. April became like a big sister to me once Lisa, Jess and I fell out. So, I told April about the conversation that I had with Trevor when we were in the guest bedroom. She was telling me that I did well to say "no" but then she said he was probably going to dump me soon because of it.

"He'll probably want someone more mature," April told me with the uttermost sincerity.

When April spoke those words, she echoed my greatest fears, I already had an inkling that Trevor was going to get bored of our relationship soon. It was inevitable, Trevor was older than me and he had older friends. I was sure that they did a lot more together than what we did. April saying that Trevor would want someone more mature just brought all of my worries to the forefront. I couldn't bear the thought of Trevor leaving me for someone else, but I didn't know what I could do about it.

April sat me down for lunch one afternoon.

"I'm eighteen years old," April began. "I have much more life experience than you Kitsu, I know what I'm talking about."

I knew that April had more life experience than me, that's why I went to her for advice, I wanted her to help me so that I didn't end up losing Trevor.

"How old is Trevor?" April asked quite bluntly.

"Well, he's seventeen," I replied.

"Right," April continued, "So what do you think goes on in the mind of a seventeen-year-old boy?"

I sighed. I knew where the conversation was going, I didn't need April to spell it out for me. Trevor was almost a grown man; he was almost eighteen years old. Trevor had so many girls that he could spend time with other than me. If I didn't keep him interested, then he was going to get bored. April wasn't necessarily telling me to go along with what Trevor wanted she was just reminding me of what would happen if I didn't. I had no idea what I was supposed to do. I wanted to run away, I wanted to run and not look back. That was my first emotion, I also wanted to bury my head in the palms of my hands and well. . . I just wanted to cry in the hope that my tears would wash the pain away. I wanted to wash away the pain of a rejection that hadn't even happened yet. The thought of Trevor leaving me was almost so unbearable I didn't even want to imagine it. I was afraid to say yes to Trevor, but I was petrified about saying no.

April had my best interests at heart, I knew she did. But I became completely paranoid after that conversation, every time I saw Trevor talking to another girl, I thought he was probably checking her out. I told myself that Trevor was bored of me and that he was going to break-up with me any minute now. To make matters worse one of the teachers at school overheard a conversation I had with April, she heard me say that I was in a boy's bedroom over the summer.

I was called out of my Science lesson during the last period to speak to one of the safeguarding team, Ms Fowler. She was a small and petite lady with a dark brown, sharp, bob-cut that swung just below her ears. Ms Fowler wasn't a teacher she was the Student Welfare Officer, she was a down-to-earth and friendly lady but us students knew not to open up to her about anything. We all knew that anything we said to Ms Fowler had the potential of being passed on to our parents.

"It's my duty," that's what Ms Fowler would say.

"I can't promise to keep anything that you tell me a secret, it's for your own good," we knew this all too well.

The conversation with Ms Fowler was so embarrassing. I had to explain everything that happened that evening, I explained that Trevor and I were only in the bedroom because we were talking about our relationship, nothing else happened. I don't know whether Ms Fowler believed me or not, but she said she was going to have to call my mother and tell her that I was in a boy's bedroom. I could already imagine how that story was going to pan out and I dreaded the thought of going home that evening. Mum didn't necessarily approve of Trevor, but she had accepted him. I didn't want anything to get in the way of the trust we had built up. I knew that mum would start worrying again once she got a call from the school. That was an understatement if ever there was one.

I got home that evening and mum started laying into me straight away. She was screaming from the top of her lungs. As soon as I opened the door, I could sense her anger, it was dominant in the atmosphere. Mum didn't even let me come fully inside the house before she started.

"In a boy's bedroom, Kitsu?"

I hung my head down, even though I knew Trevor and I didn't do anything that day, I also knew that I was contemplating it. I knew that I had discussed the possibility with April. I didn't know what to say to mum.

I started to explain the situation, but mum cut me off.

"What have I told you about keeping yourself safe?" That's how mum cut me off.

I just wanted her to listen. I wanted her to listen instead of talking. But she didn't.

Mum started the lecture again about all of these young boys only being after one thing. I told her that nothing had happened in the room with Trevor, I told her that we were just talking. Mum wasn't listening. I got really agitated that day and said a few things that I shouldn't have said.

"Why were you in the boy's bedroom?" she continued.

I didn't get to relay the whole story about how it wasn't Trevor's house it was a guest bedroom at a friend's party. I didn't see how that would have helped my situation to be quite honest. Besides, it didn't matter what I said next, mum had already done her calculations and made her decisions.

"Listen, sweetheart," mum spoke in a condescending, sympathetic tone as she delivered her heart-shattering verdict.

"You have been seeing this boy for about eight months now, I know how this story goes, all these young hormones flying around..."

Mum said that I had to stop seeing Trevor immediately because there was only a matter of time before he convinced me to do something that I might end up regretting. I couldn't believe what I was hearing. How could mum expect me to just turn around and end a relationship with a boy that I had fallen in love with? Trevor wasn't just some teenage crush or a summer fling, we had a deep lasting love.

Our relationship wasn't like a ruler that I could just snap and throw into the bin at any given moment, it was deep and real. Trevor was the beginning of the rest of my life. Mum didn't understand.

I tried to tell mum that it wasn't that simple and that I wouldn't be able to just stop seeing Trevor. But this time mum was serious. She completely banned us from speaking; once mum found out that my grades were starting to slip as well, she pretty much went cold turkey.

"This is your final year of secondary school!" Mum reminded me. "You cannot afford to let your grades slip."

I wasn't allowed to use my phone after 5 pm and I had to come straight home after school.

I know what you're thinking – did my mum really cause Trevor and I to break up? Well, mum tried to stop me from seeing Trevor, but it didn't work. Trevor didn't come around to my house to see mum again after that, but we were still very much together.

<u>Tuesday 15th September</u>

Dear Diary,

I wish I could speak to mum about Trevor. I wish that I could tell her how I feel, that way she could give me some good advice instead of just shouting at me all of the time. Mum must know how hard it is to be a teenager, she was there once herself.

This is hard. Being Trevor's girlfriend comes with its struggles, the last thing I want is to be at odd ends with mum as well. I know what would make mum happy, but I can't do it. I can't just stop seeing Trevor. Mum doesn't realise, Trevor is more than just a boy that I am seeing at secondary school; he is the love of my life.

We've been together for so long that I just can't imagine life without him. It's just not that easy to go and throw everything away.

One thing's for sure I'm not leaving Trevor and that's final.

Kitsu xoxo

Next Level?

Ok so mum was right, she said that if I stayed with Trevor for too long then I may end up doing something that I would regret. That's what happened. A month after my sixteenth birthday. Trevor and I were celebrating our first anniversary and we ended up spending the whole night together. We had been together for so long and it just seemed like the time was finally right to take things to this next level that Trevor had been so persistent about. I spoke to April and got some advice beforehand.

"Go for it," she said. "You're all grown up now."

April had left school by this point and I was coming towards the end of Year 11 - my final year of Secondary School. This was a time when I needed complete focus and no distractions, but I had gotten so wrapped up in my now 'serious relationship' with Trevor that nothing else seemed to matter to me anymore. Trevor was my life. We still had so many things that we wanted to achieve in our lives, but it was like I couldn't see that anymore. I couldn't see past my immediate surroundings - spending time with Trevor and getting to know more about him. I knew that I had changed, all of my teachers said I had changed. Their opinions didn't matter to me. All that mattered was that Trevor and I were happy love birds.

Trevor and I would often sit and talk about our future together. Believe it or not, we sat down together and planned our little family. Everyone at school saw Trevor as the rebel, the troublemaker, the menace even - but I knew the real, kind and humble side of him. I knew the real Trevor. I remember being so excited for the future that Trevor and I planned to have together.

I told Trevor about what happened with my parents, I told him that they split up when I was six years old. My dad disappeared for about five years and only contacted me for a brief moment when I turned eleven, he called me and sent me a birthday card. Even then his presence was not consistent and only disrupted my relationship with mum, so I didn't hear from him again after that. Mum said that he was trying to undermine her authority. All I knew was that I didn't want my life turning out the same way as my parents – a broken family. I wanted my future with Trevor to be secure. Trevor said that his parents were still on good terms. He didn't hear them talking that much, but when he did, they were always civil with one another. Trevor knew what it was like to come from a broken home because his parents split up when he was younger just like mine did, but Trevor didn't know what abandonment felt like because both of his parents wanted him. Trevor was happy living with his dad – they had a good relationship; he gave him so much freedom. Trevor's dad had other children as well, but they didn't live with them. Trevor also knew that our relationship was the only consistent thing that I had in my life at that point.

Mum and I didn't talk much anymore, we kind of drifted apart and mum became quite distant. Well at least that's how I saw it, but I had an inkling that she knew deep down I was still seeing Trevor and she wasn't happy about it. She never asked me though, I think the thought of me disobeying her initial instructions was something that she couldn't bear to think about. I wasn't about to bring it up either, I just got on with my relationship with Trevor quietly.

Trevor and I got over some of our early arguments about clothing and make-up. For some reason Trevor just stopped talking about it. Well, I think a lot of it was actually to do with me. I started to learn what Trevor liked and I knew how to dress in a way that would be pleasing to him. I learnt how to adapt according to his moods.

Eventually, Trevor became the perfect gentleman, he would take me out, he would always pay the bill and whenever I was cold, he would offer me his coat to wear just like the men you see in films. He acted like a grown adult even though we were only sixteen and seventeen years old. Over time I started feeling out of place at school. Everything just seemed so boring and pointless to me by this point. I started dressing differently, rolling up my school skirt so far above my knees that my thighs were practically on show at all times. That's how Trevor's friends' girlfriends all used to dress so I wanted to fit in.

I spent most of my time with Trevor, in school and out. I remember one particular day where I felt ill during school. I had my head down on the table in every lesson and I felt so tired. Some of the girls in my year at school started this horrible rumour about me, they started saying that I was pregnant and that I was going to drop out of school soon. They said that I wouldn't be able to support myself and that I would have to get a job in a local supermarket. It wasn't true, but it did make me anxious. I worried what would happen to me if I did end up pregnant. I didn't tell Trevor all of my concerns, I didn't want him to think that I was too immature to be in a relationship with him. We both agreed that we were in an adult relationship and there was no going back.

I trusted Trevor like my life depended on him, we were

joint at the hip most days. Although my grades were slipping, none of this seemed to matter much at the time. On Saturdays, Trevor would come and pick me up with one of his older friends and his girlfriend. I would get dressed up and go with Trevor to the nightclubs. Being out and about made me feel like I was in a whole new world where I could forget about all of my troubles. I loved it. If anyone asked me how I was doing I would tell them that I was having the time of my life! I would put on the cutest little skirt, 3-inch heels and a crop top – that was my weekend outfit. I made sure that my face was covered to the tee with make-up and bright red lipstick to finish off the look. That was my weekend look.

<u>Tuesday 5th April</u>

Dear Diary,

I just can't explain this feeling, the only way I know is to say that I feel invincible whenever Trevor is around. He makes my life complete; this is it for me. This is it! One day Trevor and I are going to get married. I've already decided. I'm just sitting here thinking about how much of a great husband he is going to make.

Trevor just got a new car and he's coming to pick me up to go out. I'm so excited I don't even know what to wear; I'm going to try and pick something that Trevor likes. Actually, April lent me some dresses the other day, so I'll probably just pick out one of those.

This is love, real love.

Kitsu xoxo

He's Such a Liar!

Trevor and I spent so much time together, we became almost inseparable on the weekends. There was one particular night where Trevor didn't come and pick me up, he said he wanted to go out with his boys instead. He needed some space he said. I didn't want to sound like the nagging and possessive girlfriend, so I gave him exactly what he asked for - space. I can't pretend I wasn't completely disheartened when Trevor said that because I was. I didn't know what to do with myself that night, we always spent our weekends together.

So, I called April, she was nineteen by this point and in university. I was still sixteen. April said that I could come out with her and her friends to a club that they were going to. It was for over eighteens, but April said that if I dressed myself up, I could easily pass for eighteen. So, I did. I got dressed up and April did my make-up that evening. April was good at doing make-up, she made me look like I was worth a million dollars. There was supposed to be a major event on that night, a road-block party. I had a feeling that was the same place Trevor was going to. I didn't want to go at first because I didn't want Trevor to think that I was following him around or that I didn't have a life of my own. How sad would that look, me turning up to a party that he had gone to with his friends? Nevertheless, April convinced me to go.

"It's a free country!" April kept saying.

"You're not going there for him; you're coming out with me." I listened to April because she told me what I wanted to hear at that point.

It wasn't as if Trevor and I had broken up, we were just giving each other space. I figured it wouldn't be so terrible if I turned up at the party and he saw me there. After slight deliberation, I decided to go.

Much to my devastation, I did bump into Trevor and it was the most horrific sight I had seen in my sixteen years of life! Trevor was walking through the party arm in arm with another girl. I couldn't believe my eyes. It wasn't anyone that I knew but she looked much older than me. She was covered from head to toe in make-up and cheap fake tan. She was small and petite with thick strawberry blonde hair that reached down to her lower back. Her green eyes sparkled in the club lights and her smile stretched across her entire face. Not to mention she had the most enormous fake-looking breasts I had ever seen! She must have stuffed something up her t-shirt because they looked gigantic. I couldn't believe what I was seeing. I was so angry I just wanted to walk right up to Trevor and slap him in the face, just like the women do in the movies.

April stopped me in my tracks; she didn't want me embarrassing myself, or her either for that matter. My heart sunk inside my chest; despair came over me like a dark blanket on a rainy day. Unnerving questions plagued my mind as I stood in the centre of a chaotic club surrounded by ecstatic teenagers and hoping that the ground would just swallow me up.

I didn't go over and slap Trevor that day, but I caught a

glimpse of his eye and that was enough. The look on his face said it all, it was screaming with guilt. I knew that Trevor had been up to no good. Furiously, I glared across the room at him, my eyes refusing to blink, anger rushing through my veins; I was raging, I was filled with infuriating rage. I had given Trevor the best year of my life only for me to find out that he was cheating on me with some overly made up barbie doll. I stormed out of the club as quickly as I could, unable to contain my built-up frustrations, I burst into loud, excruciating tears whilst standing on the concrete floor outside the club. I crouched down towards the ground burying my face within the palms of my hands. Every memory, everything Trevor and I had been through came racing to the forefront of my mind before settling into a tormenting glaze. Tears poured through the gaps in my fingers and soaked the ground beneath me, I wanted to throw up, the thought of Trevor and that other girl made me feel sick, I couldn't stomach it, I felt physically sick.

Trevor called me later on that evening, but I didn't answer. I didn't want to hear from him.

<u>Thursday 30th April</u>

Dear Diary,

I hear people talk about depression, but what is it? Is it more than just a dark state of mind or a place where you lose your appetite? Is it when the thought of getting out of bed in the morning brings on sudden exhaustion so that you're not motivated to do anything at all?

If that's what depression feels like, then I think I just had my first dosage. Depression is bed-ridden, and self-pity is his pillow. My heart aches when I breathe, I can't believe what's happening to me. April said I can't allow myself to feel this way. That he's just not worth it!

Kitsu xoxo

When I eventually spoke to Trevor, he reassured me that he wasn't cheating on me, he wasn't going to leave me for this other girl. Trevor said that he was just hanging out with her because he wanted a change of scenery. Change of scenery! I don't even know what came over me or why I felt like it even made sense for me to sit there listening to all of that rubbish. I guess I had gotten so used to being with Trevor that I couldn't imagine life without him anymore. I listened to whatever I had to listen to, just to keep myself sane.

I imagined myself breaking up with Trevor and I felt lonely, I felt incomplete. I entertained the thought of staying with Trevor and I felt a sense of temporary satisfaction. If I'm honest it was as though I was stuck in between a rock and the cliff upon which it hung. I felt like I had no way out. So, I stayed. I can't describe our relationship as a source of strength or happiness it was just a way of life. I guess I just accepted the state of my life. I was Trevor's girlfriend.

My self-perception wasn't the same after that day at the club. The image of Trevor and that other girl imprinted itself right there at the forefront of my mind. Convincing myself to believe Trevor was faithful and he loved me helped me to get through some days, but reality hit me once I witnessed my reflection in the mirror. When I looked at myself, I felt disgusted, my memory was branded by an impression of insufficiency. I couldn't shake off the image of the girl that I saw Trevor with at the club. Comparison had me trapped; anxiety had me bound but insecurity rendered me hopeless. I could no longer see myself for who I was, I saw myself as an insignificant version of her.

Why had Trevor lied to me that evening? Why did he tell me that he wanted to spend some time with his friends and then go out with another girl? I started to blame myself; maybe I'm not slim enough? Am I not pretty enough? Is Trevor just looking for someone more exciting? I wondered. I kept having flashbacks and mental images of the girl that I saw Trevor with, she looked alright I guess, her hair was full, long and beautiful, she had long legs and a slim waist.

But, so what? I have hair too, how did she manage to capture Trevor's attention? Led by my feelings, I started contemplating all kinds of things that I could do to recapture Trevor's affections once again. I felt like Trevor was with me, but his heart wanted to be somewhere else. Dark thoughts captured me like a prisoner behind bars. I felt like I had no way of escape. Day after day my mind was fuelled with infuriating and self-depleting thoughts. Every day I would wake up anxious and afraid. Girls at school envied my relationship with Trevor but no one knew how empty and motionless I felt on the inside.

So, I started changing the way that I looked, I got some clip in hair extensions to make sure that my hair reached to the lower part of my back just like the girls in the magazines. I started wearing a full face of make-up every day. That was until I got pulled up by the Vice-Principal; we still weren't allowed to wear make-up, not even in Year 11. I carried on wearing my make-up after that day, but I just toned it down a bit so that the teachers wouldn't notice. My new image gave me confidence, I would walk around the hallway flicking my hair back and forth, everyone complimented me on how mature I looked, and I felt so contented with myself. Once the compliments stopped and I was left alone with my thoughts I felt depressed - again. It was like I could no longer be myself anymore, I was constantly looking for signs of acceptance. My self-esteem had gone on a downward spiral.

It was May, the countdown to exams had begun but I couldn't focus on anything. I would wake up in the morning with a heavy burden on my chest. The pressure of trying to please Trevor had taken its toll on me. I stopped eating because I wanted my waist to be snatched in like the girl Trevor was with at the club. Starvation became an obsession as I fought profusely to be the perfect weight. By the end of Year 11, my grades had completely plummeted, there was no way that I was going to pass my GCSE's - I just knew it.

I remember sitting in the exam hall on the day of my final exam, it was a science paper. I sat motionless with my head cupped within the palms of my hands. The invigilator looked at me. She didn't say anything, but I felt as though she was judging me; the look in her eyes said "hopeless." Then she looked away and carried on walking around the exam hall.

"What am I doing here?" I whispered to myself as I glanced around the silent exam hall. At that point I knew that I was just in there for show, I had no idea what was going on. Even if

74

I wanted to open up the exam paper, I knew that I would have nothing to write down on the paper. I had become incapable of retaining information.

Purposeless, I sat in the packed examination hall staring at the clock. Waiting for time to pass was all that I could do at that particular moment in time. I know I shouldn't have but it happened, I had given up on myself.

Friday 25th May

Dear Diary,

I wish the ground would just swallow me up, as in right now – I feel as though I have nothing left to live for. How did this happen to me? I don't even know who I am anymore, it's like I've been robbed of myself.

I'm just going to hide underneath my duvet now. Hopefully, when I wake up, I will find out that this whole thing was just one bad dream.

Kitsu xoxo

Breaking Up

Ok, so it wasn't a dream. This was my reality. It was the summer after secondary school; I finally plucked up enough courage to break up with Trevor. I didn't have much choice, I had failed my exams and my mother was livid, she went absolutely ballistic. Almost everything that she tried to warn me against had happened and there was nothing I could say to defend myself. To make matters worse Trevor had passed his exams and finished school, guess he wasn't as irresponsible as he made himself out to be!

I was the one that had suffered the consequences of our unruliness. That made me bitter, it struck every delicate nerve in my body like a ping to a guitar string. I still didn't speak to Lisa and Jess much, but I know that they passed their exams too.

Results day was an absolute dread for me. I didn't even want to look at the transcript. I turned up there with April, I stood in the doorway watching all of the other students collect their results. Some were grinning from cheek to cheek ecstatic about their grades. Others were crying their eyes out in disappointment. Disappointment is a ball and chain around your neck, a heavy metal ball hanging on the edge of a thick, dark chain. That's how some of the other kids looked, they looked really sad. I didn't know what to think or feel, I didn't have many emotions at that point. I knew I had failed my exams and that mum was going to be so angry with me as soon as she found out. I finally plucked up enough courage to approach the transcript desk and collect my envelope. I did so with a slight snigger to convince myself that this was not a serious life-changing event. It wasn't. April stuck with me, we walked up to the collection desk together, Trevor said that he was going to collect his results later on in the afternoon and that I should let him know how it all goes.

So, there I was, the walk of shame. Ms Fowler handed me my envelope whilst looking at me straight in the eye and trying to keep a poker face, it was almost like she knew. I turned to April, then I ripped open the envelope straight away, no use lingering on it. Scanning my grades from top to bottom, I looked up at April and let out a forced laugh, "E for science," I said with a slight snigger. Pretending to be nonchalant about the whole thing, we walked towards the exit door. As soon as I got outside of my house, I just remember scribbling over my transcript with a red felt tip pen; tearing it in half and flinging it in the trash.

I couldn't even cry, I tried but no tears came out. I couldn't retrieve any source of pain, there was no reason to cry because this was the result of my own foolishness. I knew that it was a self-inflicted failure.

Later on, that afternoon, I told Trevor that we had to break everything off, if I'm completely honest I still wasn't over the whole cheating ordeal; finding out that Trevor was going off to college whilst I hadn't even finished school was just too much shame to bare. I could only imagine what he would be getting up to at college. It was for the best, I decided.

Trevor looked ecstatic, that day, his eyes glistening with

delight and his smile beaming from one side of his face to the other – I didn't even think that Trevor cared about school like that. Guess I got that one wrong, well Trevor had us all fooled. He said he had plans with his dad that evening, they were going out to celebrate his results. I didn't even want to think about mum, I hadn't seen her that day yet. Trevor tried to be sympathetic towards me, but it didn't even matter anymore. It was enough. I was a complete blubbering mess during that conversation, I think the only words I managed to blurt out were "I can't do this anymore," and "My mum is going to kill me." I couldn't see past my nose anymore. Woken up by the sweet stench of reality, I couldn't see beyond myself, this was my life.

Trevor didn't say much during the conversation, he pretty much let me speak until I was done sobbing and wailing then that was it – he walked off. Trevor said that he wanted to go out and 'test the waters anyway' whatever that meant. I remember standing there for a while after Trevor had disappeared from sight, there I stood staring aimlessly into the distance doubting myself and wondering whether I had made the right decision. Trevor walked away and he didn't look back. Not even once.

Not long after my breakup with Trevor, depression hit me again, this time it was much more intense. This second bust of depression was a black cloud, it hung low above my head and was ready to erupt at any moment. April said that I was having withdrawal symptoms, I had been with Trevor for the better part of two years and now to just be torn apart in one sudden instance was virtually unbearable. I didn't expect it to hurt that much but it did. I couldn't confide in mum that much because she had already made her feelings clear, she warned me about my relationship with Trevor and I didn't listen. I only had myself to blame. I didn't know what else to do.

Wrestling with thoughts of inferiority was my greatest torment. I woke up feeling low as the ground beneath me; I went to bed with a draining sensation that stemmed from my constant mind battles. Walking away from Trevor wasn't easy but going back seemed just as daunting. Fighting, struggling and wrestling for my sanity made me feel like a woman chasing after her own shadow – purposeless. The next few months of my life seemed endless, monotonous and pitiful. They say love hurts but I never expected it to be so agonising. I didn't go back to Trevor, but I didn't fully regain my sense of self either. The image of the girl I compared myself to had arrested my self-esteem. I found myself doing things that I never thought that I would do.

<u>Monday 31st August</u>

Dear Diary,

I don't even know who I am any more. Ok so I'm no longer Trevor's girlfriend and that's fine but I guess I can still be me. The only thing is, I don't think I know how to do that anymore. Who am I? I spent so long being who Trevor wanted me to be, I don't know how to be me. I've had enough, of feeling like this. I just want to look different, feel different and be someplace else other than where I am right now.

It felt weird today walking down the street by myself without Trevor next to me. But I can do this I know that I can. I just need something new. A new look, a new image and then everything will be ok again.

I feel so liberated, time for me to focus on myself now...

Kitsu xoxo

The next few months of my life were different, to say the least. Instead of researching college courses and new career paths, I found myself researching how to get breast implants. That was me, sixteen years old, thinking about how I could get myself breast implants. I was no longer doing this to please Trevor, I just felt as though I were only a shell of who I used to be, nothing I did seemed good enough anymore. I had enough of being Kitsu, I wanted to be someone else. That's when I built up the wall, I decided that I was never going to let anyone deceive me or take me for a fool ever again.

I Want Breast Implants

The next year of my life consisted of me saving up thousands of pounds to get myself some breast implants. I got in contact with a private surgery up in Baker Street, they said I had to wait until I was at least eighteen years old before I could have the operation done. I didn't want to wait a whole year but at least it gave me enough time to save up. I told mum that I hadn't decided what I wanted to do career-wise and so I wanted to take a year out and decide. Ironically, I managed to get a job in a local supermarket, that's how I managed to save up enough money for what I needed to do. It took me almost a year to save up enough money for the operation, working in the supermarket didn't do that much for my self-esteem but at least it got me out of bed in the morning.

Then the day finally came. It was a cold day, much like any other early winter. The trees were bare and leafless. Birds flew aimlessly through the breezy sky and a subtle mist filled the atmosphere. Peace. Tranquillity. Calmness protruded even from the ground beneath me. I didn't tell anyone about my appointment at the surgery, this was something that I had to do by myself and for myself. So, I got off the Tube just outside of Baker Street Station and strolled through the empty air, inhaling the sweet scent of my surroundings. All of this was about to erupt; the calmness was moments away from chaos. I continued my lonesome stroll, seeing the double glass doors of the surgery in the distance.

I was greeted by a tall, slim, receptionist called Suzie. She didn't tell me her name; I could see it on her badge. Suzie looked like she had breast implants as well. I was able to notice these things because I had spent so much time researching. Suzie gave me some paperwork to complete and asked me to take a seat in the waiting room until I was called. I sat in the waiting room for a few minutes tapping my fingers together and trying not to talk myself out of it. I had come too far to give up.

"Miss Kitsu Bolton!" said a sweet, delicate voice. I looked up and my heart skipped a beat. "You're next," the lady continued. That was it – time to go.

Before I knew it, I found myself sitting in a whitewashed room surrounded by surgeons and their face masks. I felt as though my whole life was about to spring up and elevate into a whole new level of fabulous. I was ready. The instruments were steel and polished, the room was silent, save for the sound of my heart pumping with excessive speed. The time had come, the chopping and changing that was about to transform me into a whole new level of confidence. Drowsily, I lay on the flat surgery bed; dressed in a pale, blue, hospital-style gown. The local anaesthetic began to kick in; I could feel my eyes closing and my senses switching off one at a time. Nervousness crept up on me for a slight moment as I pondered on whether or not I was making the right decision. I began contemplating how I had ended up in this situation. I asked myself when life got so complicated; before I could answer my thoughts, I sunk into a deep sleep.

The next thing I remember was sitting in a recovery room, with a bruising and swelling around the area where the surgery had taken place. I thought I would feel much better about myself after the breast implants.

I didn't.

I remember a kind and soft-spoken nurse telling me that the pain would go away within a few weeks and that I would feel much better. The pain submerged. I didn't feel any better. Furthermore, I became slightly obsessed with my new implants, I kept checking them in the mirror as I didn't think that they were the same size. They seemed uneven.

I remember one particular afternoon, early spring, it was warm outside and even hotter inside, I couldn't think straight because of the heat. Mum had gone to work, and it was just me in the house. That's when I started scrolling, I went on Instagram to look at all of the celebrities I knew that had gone through breast enhancement surgery. They looked amazing. I felt nauseated, looking at them filled me with nausea – I felt the same way I did when I first saw Trevor with that overly made-up girl in the club. You know how some people say that procrastination is the thief of time? Well comparison is an even bigger thief of time – and energy. Comparison is an experienced robber; she'll snatch away your sense of self-worth and make you forget everything that you were before you met her.

Immersed in my thoughts, I began to dream. Even in my newly formed figure I still dreamt about the things I wished I had. Hours, I spent hours looking at these women and their perfect bodies, toned stomachs, sculpted legs and skin void of blemishes.

Every day I would wake up, stare at my reflection in the mirror and then flick back through the Instagram posts. I could have almost sworn that my left breast implant was bigger than the right – they looked so odd. I felt like I had lob sided breasts and I couldn't wear fitted tops anymore. I was so conscious that someone else would notice. When I called the surgery to enquire about my different sized implants, they reassured me that it was impossible. They said that I should stop over analysing myself and that it was all in my head. I spoke to a really pleasant receptionist who offered to arrange a post-treatment check-up with one of the nurses. It wasn't their usual procedure, but she could tell that I was worried.

I didn't want to spend too much time going back and forth with the surgery; I didn't want to alert any additional attention to myself considering I had already lied about my age during our initial consultation. I politely declined.

"Not to worry. You'll get used to them," replied the quiet, squeaky voice on the other side of the phone.

"If you change your mind then just give us a call back." I didn't call back again after that, I just tried to accept it.

<u>Thursday 2nd March</u>

Dear Diary,

OK so this morning I checked again, and I could swear the left one is bigger. It doesn't look right – I wonder whether other people have noticed as well.

It's so strange though when I look at other women with these designer bodies, they look so content, so confident and happy with themselves. They're always smiling in the pictures. I wonder whether I am the only woman with breast implants who still hates her figure.

They feel so uncomfortable as well.

I haven't eaten much today because I've been so busy obsessing over these breasts of mine. Argh, this is not what I signed up for.

Right, enough is enough I need to stop and tell myself to get a grip.

Kitsu, get a grip!

Kitsu xoxo

Mother-Daughter Bonds

When mum found out about my breast implants, she didn't say much at all, she just sighed. It was as if she had given up fighting. Or maybe she knew that this was something that I had to do for myself. It was really obvious that my self-esteem had dropped, and I guess mum noticed it as well. She didn't say much to me about anything, I didn't know which reaction I would have preferred to be honest.

My relationship with mum started to get a bit distant after a while, I didn't tell her much because I didn't have much to say. We saw each other in the house; it became like we were living together but we weren't spending that much time together. We were almost like housemates, instead of a mother and daughter living under the same roof. The distance got a lot better once the awkwardness died down and mum got used to my new body image. That's how I wanted it, no arguments, no long discussions, just acceptance.

Eventually, Mum got a new job that meant she had to take a secondment to Taiwan for three months. A secondment is when your workplace sends you to another company for a few months – kind of like an internship except you're not an intern. Mum had become a senior associate at her Law firm.

Did I mention that mum is a solicitor? She wasn't always one, after dad left mum was down and depressed for a long time. Mum worked at Sainsbury's as a cashier. I could tell that she wasn't happy because she always spoke about how she could have been doing so much more with her life. I blamed myself for mums seeming unhappiness most of the time. I just thought that if she never had me to look after then she would have been doing so much more with her life. Mum never made me feel like I was holding her back, these were just my thoughts.

When I turned twelve, mum went back to complete her Legal Practice Course and eventually became a solicitor at a large conveyancing firm. I always knew that mum was clever, she told me that my dad always used to put her down and make her feel as though she couldn't amount to much. I think mum was glad when he left. It was difficult for me, but I think that mum preferred it. I was glad to see mum getting on with her own life for once. Finally, she was focusing on herself. I was eighteen at this point anyway, old enough to look after myself.

I had a feeling that mum had met someone, she didn't tell me, not in so many words but I just knew. It was like her persona had changed. Mum called me every week whilst she was in Taiwan just to check up on me and see how I was doing. She never mentioned that she had met anyone, but I just knew she had.

Shortly after mum travelled to Taiwan, I got a new job in a salon near our house. This wasn't what I had planned for my life, but I had to do something to get away from the thoughts inside of my head and away from looking at my reflection in the mirror. My manager at the salon was nice, her name was Nancy. Nancy was an old lady, frail but full of life. She didn't style hair anymore, but she came in now and then to check on the business.

Nancy was so inspirational, you could tell that she had worked hard her whole life, her eyes had depth, they had seen things I could only dream of; her words had wisdom they had come from places I've probably never even set foot upon. When Nancy spoke her voice naturally commanded the attention of the room. Every time Nancy visited the hair salon, she greeted me and asked me questions about my life.

"Do you know what you want to do yet?" Nancy enquired with attentive ears.

When Nancy said that what she meant was: "Do I know what I want to do with the rest of my life?"

Even though I was working at the salon, I knew that this wasn't it for me. This was never my, 'Plan A.' Nancy so badly wanted to help me. I didn't do much in the salon, I just washed the customers hair and did some blow-drying. The simple stuff. But it was enough to get me out of bed in the morning and it was enough to get me by. Besides, I needed a change of scenery from the local supermarket.

There was this one day that Nancy came in and we had a long conversation. She said she wanted to help me get my life in order and that she believed I could go far. Like I said, Nancy was a great and inspiring speaker. Nancy's belief in me helped me to believe in myself.

"You're a young girl," Nancy would remind me.

"You've got your whole life ahead of you, the world is your oyster."

Nancy always gave such great advice; she spoke words that could uplift me out of my downtrodden state of mind. Nancy's words gave me so much hope. Nancy wasn't an ordinary woman; she was a devout Christian woman, she lived by the Word of

God. Nancy would always come into the salon with a large smile spread across her face - no matter what time of day.

One day Nancy spoke to me and it was like she could hear my thoughts. I didn't say anything to her; I don't think I spoke out loud either. We were in between customers and I was sitting alone on the soft corner sofa with my eyes staring at a blank page in my diary. I couldn't write anything in my diary back then; I went through a phase where it felt like my thoughts were stuck inside of my head. They would no longer pour onto the page as before. I couldn't call it writer's block because it wasn't like I was writing a story. So, I called it an emotional block. I was finding it difficult to express my emotions. All I had was questions.

That's when Nancy came and whispered to me:

"Created to worship," that's what she said.

"You were created to worship God."

Nancy told me that I was selling myself short, she said that I should let the past go and make the most of every opportunity. At that point, I was going in and out of what can only be described as bouts of depression. I thought I had covered it up well. I always tried to make myself look busy to take my mind off of it, but Nancy knew. She just knew. Regret is a grey cloud, heavy and transparent.

"He's such an idiot!" I would blurt out every time I thought about Trevor and everything he had put me through.

"He's such a waste of space."

Nancy told me that I had to let it go, she said that I had to stop thinking negative thoughts about Trevor and that I had to stop putting my life on hold.

It was like I was stuck in the same fifteen-year-old state of mind even though almost three years had passed by since I last spoke to Trevor.

"You're better than this," that was one of the last things I remember Nancy saying to me before I left the salon.

The strange thing about Nancy was that I don't think she spoke to anyone else as much as she spoke to me. And I was just the salon helper, it felt good to know that someone had noticed me though. Nancy made me think positive thoughts about myself, she challenged me to think big and to never settle.

Friday 2ⁿᵈ June

Dear Diary,

Tonight, I cried. I didn't just sob and sulk, but I cried tears, real tears.

I wanted to cry so bad because I wanted the tears to carry the pain away – I can't shake this feeling and I've tried so hard. My heart feels heavy and my mind feels even heavier.

I've been running the same situations through my mind for the past three years now. Every time I run away the memories seem to catch right back up with me again.

I don't want to see Trevor when I close my eyes; I don't want to see another girl's face when I look at myself in the mirror. I don't want to be tied down by the pressure of comparison and I don't want to feel angry anymore.

I just want to be me again.

I'm tired of pretending and putting on a brave face, I need help. I need somebody to HELP ME!

Kitsu xoxo

Making Up For Lost Time

Sitting in the corner of an empty café with my thoughts swirling around inside a cup of decaffeinated tea, that's when it finally hit me. All that Nancy was trying to say and do was all starting to make sense. I was nineteen years old, no education, no boyfriend, low self-esteem and a breast implant operation that had gone wrong. Reality hit me like a boulder weight smacking itself repeatedly against my forehead. It was time for me to GET MY LIFE IN ORDER!

I didn't know what to do back then, there were so many things in my life that had gone wrong, but I just thought it was best to focus on the things that were within my control and let the rest just simply fall into place.

The wall that I built up was still going strong, I wasn't letting anyone close to me – I couldn't risk falling back into as low a state as I was in when I just broke up with Trevor.

I never knew what heartache felt like until I met Trevor. There are some experiences in life that I would just have rather gone without. I wish I never had to know what heartbreak felt like! It's a horrible state of being, you feel like you just can't function, it's less like a physical pain and more of an emotional strain. Heartbreak feels like an emptiness in your chest that travels up into your mind and causes everything around you to seem distant and motionless. All I knew was that I didn't want that feeling of emptiness to come back to me again. I didn't want to feel that low ever again in my life. The only way I knew to avoid that from happening, was to keep everyone out. So, like a candle in the stagnant, open-air, I continued to burn without falter or effect – I decided that no one was going to drag me down that low ever again.

So, it was coming up to the summer months; it was time for me to get my life in order and I knew it all too well. I started applying for colleges. I didn't have much hope of getting a better job without some form of education under my belt; nevertheless, I started my search.

Discouragement swindled me at the start, I was limited in my choices because I didn't have enough GCSE's. I managed to scrape a 'C' in my art exam but that was about it. I didn't even have the basics – English and Maths – the basics. It wasn't easy, not at all and I got a lot of rejection letters; that didn't mean it was impossible though. I knew that it was going to be a long and difficult journey ahead, but I was prepared for it. Well, as best prepared as I could've been.

Rejection is a hard pill to swallow; it's tube-shaped, sugar-coated and gets stuck like a lump in your throat. Seriously, rejection is a hard pill to swallow!

<u>Wednesday 14th July</u>

Dear Diary,

I don't know if I can take any more of these rejection letters. I know I don't have many GCSE's but I'm trying.. I really am trying.

Speaking to April doesn't seem to make a difference. It's weird because I still keep the wall up around her, she just seems to have a way of peering over it and gaining access – not complete access though. April says that she got many rejection letters when she applied to college as well, but she never gave up. I don't know what else to do, I guess I just have to keep going.

No one knows what goes on in my head. I mean I can't tell April everything...can I?

Kitsu xoxo

Eventually, I managed to find a college course where I could retake my English and Maths GCSE's whilst doing an apprenticeship. Fortunately for me, I managed to enrol onto an intermediate level Art and Design apprenticeship. At least it was something that I had a passion for, and it allowed me to express myself once again.

So, there I was nineteen years old, in college and trying to get my life back together again. I was just trying to regain some sense of self. Art was my favourite subject at school, I was doing so well in it until I met Trevor and got off track. I was excited to know that I had been offered a place on the course and I couldn't wait to start. I told myself that this was the year when everything was going to come together.

I remember when I started at the college, I enjoyed my course but there was still something that didn't feel quite right. I just didn't feel completely satisfied. I didn't know what it was.

I didn't make many friends at college; it was weird. I felt out of place because most people there were younger than me. It wasn't a major age gap, just a few years or so but sometimes I felt as though I didn't belong. In my mind, they all knew that I was older than them and I didn't belong there. Some days I felt ready; focused; on top of the world. Other days I just wanted to climb into bed and bury myself underneath my duvet with a hot cup of cocoa.

I was home alone most afternoons as well because mum had gone travelling for work, well at least that's what she told me. It became even more obvious that mum had met someone out in Taiwan because she kept saying she had news for me, and she wanted me to fly over there, but I couldn't because I was at college.

<u>Monday 19th September</u>

Dear Diary,

It feels so good to finally be doing something productive with my life. I feel like I can be me once again. At least I have some sense of direction and something to keep my mind off of all that has happened.

It gets lonely sometimes without mum being around but I'm not going to sit here and sob because I don't think she's thinking about me much. She's probably having the time of her life in Taiwan.

I haven't made many friends at college; well I haven't made any in fact – I think I prefer it this way. I'm happy that I'm on the right path and doing something constructive but I just wish I could be free, like really be free from the pain of my past. It's hard because I'm reminded of it every time I look in the mirror.

Why did I do this to myself? Why did I get these fake breasts? Oh yes. I remember why, and I want to cry all over again.

Kitsu xoxo

I Met Bodel

College was much different to being at Secondary School. We had a lot more freedom and independence. I kept myself to myself; I preferred it that way. I did miss having a group of friends though, like how it was at Secondary School. But when I thought about all of the drama with Jess and Lisa, I changed my mind again. I decided to stay within the constraints of my wall.

I tried hard to keep people out of my life but at times I started to feel lonely. I didn't have anyone to share my daily struggles with – well other than my diary of course.

Eventually, I met a girl at college who was part of the Christian Union, she was down to earth and understanding. Her name was Bodel, she was eighteen years old and finishing off her A-levels. There was something about Bodel that was just different to anyone else I had met at college. The other girls I met at college were just interested in going out to parties and meeting up with boys. I just didn't want to do that anymore. Most evenings I just wanted to be home and curled up with a nice cup of hot cocoa and my pillow – guess all that time I spent with Nancy had rubbed off on me. Besides, I just didn't want a repeat of my school days. I didn't want to get distracted by a boy; fall in love; experience heartbreak and end up in a state of depression. Not again!

Bodel wasn't into parties either she was focused on her work, we also had a few things in common because Bodel was into Art and Design just like I was. She wanted to become an Interior Designer one day. We ate lunch together and we sat down and spoke about our dreams and goals. I wouldn't say I completely let my walls down, but Bodel seemed like someone I could talk to.

I remember opening up to Bodel about how I messed my life up in Secondary School all because of a boy. This was the first time I spoke to someone about Trevor in almost four years. I thought I had moved so far past him but when I started talking and recollecting the situation it was as though that very same pain, those very same memories came flooding back to the surface. I felt like I was reliving it all over again – so I stopped talking.

I told Bodel that mum had moved to Taiwan with a guy she met at work and that she had married him. I didn't go to the wedding because I had college work to focus on. That was all I said about my family life, Bodel never asked me about my father so I didn't bring him up. I think my silence said enough though. I didn't tell Bodel anything else about my life except that I was trying to get it back together since leaving Secondary School. Bodel didn't say much in response at first but she looked at me with eyes of understanding.

"I know what it's like to feel alone," Bodel replied with an empathetic expression.

Bodel told me about her experiences in Secondary School and her family. She told me that she didn't know her birth mother because her birth mother had died during childbirth. Bodel was being brought up by her adoptive parents Luis and

Maddie, who had taken her in as their very own. Bodel told me that story with such a straight disposition, almost devoid of any emotions. She said she met her biological father once in her life and that was about three years ago. I didn't know what to say. I felt like I had been through trauma, but it was nothing compared to what I was hearing.

The strange thing about Bodel was that she spoke about weighty things as if they were light. She spoke about things that could leave a burn mark as if they had only left a scratch. Bodel was bold, she wasn't like anyone I had met before. She was bodacious and confident; I wanted to be just like her.

"Whatever happened to your dad?" Bodel asked me one afternoon during lunch. I found her boldness quite intriguing. Most people would feel as though they had to walk on eggshells with difficult and sensitive topics like not having a father, but Bodel was different, she just asked. So, I told her.

"I haven't seen him in over ten years," I replied with an exhale and a look of disappointment both at the same time. I had gotten so used to my father not being around that it almost seemed pointless to even talk about him.

I remember hanging my head down when I said this. I hung my head down and took a deep breath because talking about my father uncovered wounds that had never really healed. I wasn't able to talk about my father in the same way that Bodel spoke about her father because thinking about him made me feel heavy-hearted and on the brink of depression again. I don't even know which cord strikes a heavier blow, the pain of heartache or the pain of knowing that your father left you as a child and hasn't come back since.

"Thirteen years, that's how long I haven't seen him for," saying it aloud like that made it seem so real to me.

I knew my father had left mum and I when I was a child, but blocking out the abandonment helped me to block out the pain that came along with it. Then I thought about Trevor, he knew all about my father. Trevor knew about all that I had been through. It was almost like he tore off the bandage of abandonment only to cover it with a plaster.

I asked Bodel how she did it. I wanted to know how she managed to deal with so much pain and disappointment in her life and still stand so strong.

"I AM taught me," that was her first response.

"I'm sorry did you say, Ryan?" I reacted with squinted eyes.

"No, I said I AM," Bodel repeated herself with a slight smirk. She must have known how weird this whole thing sounded.

"I AM? What kind of strange name is that?!" I exclaimed.

Bodel sniggered again at my reaction.

"Oh sorry, does sound a bit strange doesn't it?"

"A bit?" I looked searchingly at Bodel waiting for an explanation, this was starting to sound really weird.

"I'm talking about God – I use I AM as a nickname for God."

"Why is that?' I asked.

"Well," Bodel took a deep breath. "A few years ago, I was in a dark place, a really dark place. I was suffering from rejection, abandonment and resentment amongst other things. I was messed up Kitsu, I didn't even know who I was."

I looked at Bodel without blinking. She didn't relent.

"But then I got to know God. When God showed me who He was, that's when I got to know who I am. That's why I call Him I AM."

Bodel took a short pause, she could see how engrossed I was in her explanation. I kept silent and listened.

"But the point is Kitsu," Bodel continued. "You need to know Jesus. It's through Him and Him alone that you can be free. That emptiness that you feel, that longing that you feel to be complete, it's because you need Jesus. It was through Jesus Christ that I got saved and delivered from the pain of the past.

That's what you asked me about right? You wanted to know how I dealt with the pain of my past?"

This time I nodded and Bodel continued.

"Well Kitsu, God says that if you confess with your mouth that Jesus is Lord and believe in your heart that God raised Him from the dead, you will be saved. That's what I did. I asked Jesus to come into my heart. Once I accepted Jesus into my heart, He healed me from the pain of the past. He taught me how to love myself."

Bodel looked at me with both child-like innocence and adult sincerity.

"I found my identity in Christ, Kitsu I found my identity in Jesus."

I was starting to understand Bodel a bit more at that point. I had heard about Jesus through some of the nativity plays I did as a child.

"Ok, so are you talking about the baby Jesus?" I enquired.

"I'm talking about the Man, Christ Jesus – God's only begotten Son."

Bodel began to break it down for me.

"God sent Jesus into this world so that through Him we might receive forgiveness of our sins and so that we could be saved. When I accepted Jesus into my heart He showed me who I was in Him. He opened my eyes Kitsu, he gave me a new life in Him. That's why I no longer feel broken and tormented because of my past."

I could feel a tear forming in the corner of my eye as I listened to Bodel speak about the Man, Christ Jesus that came into her heart and changed her life. I looked at her with a wordless expression; I could feel my insides bubbling up almost like they wanted to explode. As Bodel spoke, I felt my own life flash before my eyes. I couldn't silence my thoughts. I wanted to know whether Jesus could give me a new life too.

After Bodel had spoken those words, she paused and looked at me waiting for a response.

I paused for the longest minute. I wished to be healed from the pain of the past as well. I really did. I wanted what Bodel had. I wanted to know that same Jesus that Bodel knew.

Bodel spoke again and just like with Nancy, I felt as though she could hear my thoughts. She could hear me replaying all the things that I wished for.

"You can be saved too Kitsu, you can have a new life in Jesus too."

I was too overwhelmed to speak. Silently, I looked at Bodel and nodded.

"God says that if you confess with your mouth that Jesus is Lord and believe in your heart that God raised Him from the dead, you will be saved."

I pondered on those words for a moment.

"Do you believe this Kitsu?"

I didn't know much about Jesus but I knew that what Bodel was telling me was real; I could see that there was something different in her. I finally managed to swallow my admiration and speak.

"Yes, I believe it."

Bodel said that if I wanted to meet Jesus then she could lead me to Him with a prayer.

She took my hands in hers and led me in a prayer.

That was the day that I gave my life to Jesus.

I felt like a huge weight had been lifted off of my shoulders; I didn't know how to process it. It was almost like a hard turtle shell had cracked from my back and began to fall away piece by piece. I could stand up straight, I could walk quickly, and I could exhale as if oxygen had been trapped in my lungs for several years.

Bodel told me that I could speak to God the same way

that I spoke to her. I could talk to Him openly and He would answer me.

"I don't talk to people that much Bodel, I usually just write my thoughts down in my diary."

Bodel gave another slight snigger.

"God's thoughts are recorded in His journal too."

"God has a journal?" I asked in ignorance.

Bodel reached inside her bag and pulled out a slim book with a brown leather cover, the pages were thin; some were covered with pink and yellow highlighter pen. Bodel held the book towards me.

'Is that the Holy Bible?" I asked.

"Yes, all of God's thoughts are recorded in this journal, the Bible. This is how God speaks to me, through His thoughts; through His Word."

I was in awe once again.

"Can I have conversations with God?" I wondered aloud. Bodel interrupted my thoughts with her kindness.

"This is my Bible, but I have a spare one that you can have." Bodel smiled as she handed me the Bible.

"Thank you." I replied in gratitude.

"God's journal, God has a journal." I repeated this under my breath, whilst graciously tucking my neatly wrapped Bible away in my handbag.

I went home that evening and I did what Bodel said I should do. I wrote letters to God in my diary; I read the Bible and I wrote down the words that I heard back in response. That year I learnt that I could have conversations with God. I could speak to God; not only that but God began to speak back to me. I recorded every word He said; I wrote it down in my diary.

<u>Tuesday 3rd December</u>

Dear God,

Thank you for accepting me into Your family.

I want to know how I can let go of my past because sometimes when I close my eyes, I remember the things that have happened and I feel really low. I guess I never should have gotten involved with Trevor in the first place. God, I know that some of my pain is self-inflicted. But I remind myself that you have forgiven me, and I remind myself of Your words God.

You said that if we confess our sins, You are faithful and just to forgive us our sins and to cleanse us from all unrighteousness. – 1 John 1:19

This means that you have blotted out my wrongdoings, so that You can concentrate on seeing the good in me, right? I just need to forgive myself now, I need to shake off the painful memories.

God, can you heal me like you healed those people in the Bible? Can you heal me from the pain of the past?

I have many scars Lord, the scars that my father left me with when he abandoned us; the scars that my mother left me with when she absconded to Taiwan and the heartbreak that Trevor caused me whilst I was at Secondary School. I gave up everything for him. Each time I glance at myself in the mirror it's just a reminder of how much I lost myself just to keep him.

God, can you help me to be me again? Bodel told me that You are a Healer. God, can you heal me from the pain of the past?

Kitsu xoxo

> *"Come to Me, all you who labor and are heavy laden, and I will give you rest. Take My yoke upon you and learn from Me, for I am gentle and lowly in heart, and you will find rest for your souls." – Matthew 11:28-29*

The next few months of my life consisted of me writing intimate letters to God within the pages of my journal. I came to realise that holding on to painful memories is tiring, draining and burdensome. I needed to let go. I told myself that in Christ I am a new creation, old things have passed away and all things have become new. If you don't release painful memories and leave space for healing, then the memories will eat away at everything in your present; maybe even your future. Each time I wrote my feelings down in my journal I felt a weight being lifted off of my shoulders. Each time I wrote a letter to God in my journal I would pause and listen afterwards in complete silence. Then I would write down the words that I heard back from God that day. I wanted to know how I would know when God was speaking to me and when I was hearing my thoughts. Bodel told me that whenever God speaks to her, His words align up with what is written in the Bible. The more I started reading my Bible the more that I got used to recognising when God was speaking to me.

When I went back to college day after day, I would speak to Bodel and she would ask me how everything was going. I felt like I was getting stronger and stronger each day. Eventually, I started going to church with Bodel. Everything was starting to fall back into place, and I was becoming me again.

At lunchtimes, Bodel and I would sit down and pray together, it wasn't the same prayer that I prayed the first time, each one was different, each one was unique. When Bodel and I sat down to pray I felt like I was having conversations - real-life conversations - with God.

If there ever was a deep black hole burning through the middle of my heart, I could no longer feel it. It was replaced with a lightness and an airy feeling, I started to feel whole and complete for the first time in years. I knew that I had been forgiven, I knew that I was free.

That Old Rugged Past

Just when I had gotten my life back on track, I was nineteen years old, in college and retaking my exams, the past reared its ugly head like a fiery-eyed, clawless monster.

It was Trevor, coming back into my life once again. I bumped into Trevor by accident.

Isn't it funny how just when you're no longer looking for something, that's when you find it?

I was just walking in Greenwich High Street on a Saturday afternoon, looking for a quiet place to sit down and catch up on some artwork. I had loads to do that day and I just wanted to get it done without any disturbances. I perched myself in the corner of a quiet little café in the middle of Greenwich Park. It was surrounded by trees, lakes and greenery. The perfect place to find some much-needed inspiration. As I sat there with my cup of Chai Tea and my art sketchbook opened on a double page, I began to breathe in the fresh Autumn air. The moment I exhaled and looked down at my page I saw a shadow from the corner of my eye.

I turned around and it was Trevor. I didn't expect to see

him, not at all. As I said it was a quiet little café, tucked away in the corner of a discreet area of Greenwich Park.

Trevor must have followed me, I concluded. He must have seen me walking down the main high street and followed me. I didn't invite him to sit down so he stood looking at me not saying anything for a while. I looked up and smiled, anticipating what his next move was going to be.

"Hi Kitsu," he began.

"Hi." I gave Trevor short answers so as not to invite any further conversation.

"What brings you here?" Trevor continued.

At this point I just took a deep sigh and looked around; it was pretty obvious what I was doing there. I was sat overlooking a picturesque landscape, I had my art sketchbook out and my charcoal pencils spread across the table. Then all of sudden, Trevor came and stood right next to my table in full obstruction of my beautiful scenery.

"Just catching up on some work," I didn't give Trevor any more information than was necessary.

"Well, it's really good to see you," Trevor spoke with the same cheeky grin that he had when we first met all those years ago, at secondary school. To Trevor, it was as if he was just catching up with an old-time friend. To me, it was as if something I had erased from my life was trying to re-surface itself again.

I didn't feel anger or resentment towards Trevor, but I didn't feel compassion or excitement towards him either. I didn't feel anything, it was like I just went numb. I felt nothing. I answered all of Trevor's questions in a monotonous tone, whilst secretly hoping that he would just go away. I couldn't look him in the eyes for too long though – just in case. I hadn't seen Trevor for so long and I'd gotten so used to being away from him that I didn't want any old feelings to come back.

I was curious though, so I asked Trevor what he was doing in the area.

"What brings you back around here?"

I figured that Trevor would have been off at University in Nottingham by now. Trevor always said that he wanted to travel for University and get away from living at home.

"Just came by to see some mates. I'm just down here for the weekend." Trevor replied still standing just inches away from my table.

We made a bit of small talk for a few minutes and then Trevor started acting like he was in a major rush to go somewhere. That's when he brought out his phone and put it on the table right next to my charcoal crayons.

"I've got to go but let's swap numbers and catch up soon." Trevor slipped that comment in the same sly and complacent way he always did. Like he just expected me to want to get back in contact with him again.

Trevor started smirking at me. It was the same way he looked at me when we first met almost five years ago; only this time when Trevor smirked, it wasn't cute. I felt sick. If I had a bucket next to me, I would've ducked my head down and thrown up. I felt physically sick! I could sense Trevor's lying, deceitful aura, it was plastered all over his face - Trevor was trying to entangle me into his web of lies all over again. I only had to gaze down at my chest to remember how far getting involved with Trevor had gotten me the last time. Trevor probably even had another girlfriend for all that I knew.

He was so convincing though. Trevor was a master manipulator. I bet he had even more years of experience under his belt after going off to college for a couple of years, not to mention being away at university. I had no idea what Trevor was capable of doing.

Trevor pulled out a chair and sat down for a moment, he

looked into my eyes with an appearance of sincerity, that's when he began to spew his venom. Trevor told me that he missed me and that letting me walk out of his life was the biggest mistake that he's ever made. His words were few, then he paused for a long moment as if in deep contemplation. During the pause, I was almost convinced, and I almost believed him, and I almost shed a tear. But I didn't.

"How's mum?" Trevor changed the subject whilst waiting for me to type my number into his phone. At this point, his phone was still sitting quite uncomfortably on the table next to my charcoal crayons.

Trevor would always make subtle remarks like that, he would remove personal pronouns from people who were close to me, as a way of making me feel like he cared about me. He wanted me to feel like my mother was his mother; that would mean he was a really important person in my life. I didn't realise that Trevor was being so cunning at the time, but I could see it so clearly in that moment. Trevor hadn't changed. He was just being himself. He was just the same seventeen-year-old boy with a taller body and more facial hair.

I smiled at Trevor for a second and in my mind, I imagined myself picking up his phone and placing my phone number inside of it. I pictured myself handing the phone back to Trevor saying bye to him and then watching him walk out of that cafe with a grin of satisfaction. That's what I imagined myself doing, but I didn't do that.

Instead, I just looked at Trevor looked at the phone and then handed his phone back to him whilst shaking my head very subtly.

Trevor carried on smiling as he understood what the subtle shaking of the head meant. I could tell that it wasn't a response he was used to. I could describe Trevor's reaction as arrogance, but that doesn't even seem fitting. Oftentimes what we perceive as arrogance is just a cover-up for insecurity within a person. I realise now, that moment wasn't even about me, it was about him. Trevor didn't care about me, not really, Trevor didn't care about anyone, he just needed that attention, he needed that validation of knowing that he was wanted. He wanted to know that even after all of these years he could just click his fingers and I would just come running straight back into his life; straight back into the pit from which I had escaped. I wasn't going to make it that easy, I wasn't going to give Trevor that satisfaction.

"Oh, you don't want to keep in touch with me?" Trevor asked whilst reaching for his phone. Trevor spoke quietly, looking around with a slightly shocked expression upon his face.

"No, we don't need to swap numbers, Trevor," I spoke assertively whilst trembling on the inside.

Trevor looked at me for a second. It was almost as if he expected me to burst out laughing and tell him that I was just joking; of course, we should swap numbers and meet up again as soon as possible. I didn't do that though. This time I had enough courage to tell Trevor, "No," and not look back.

Trevor turned around and walked out of the café with a perplexed look on his face. I was glad to have escaped from Trevor's clutches, but I must admit, seeing him again after all of those years shook me up a bit. I couldn't concentrate on my artwork straight after Trevor left the café. It was like something daunting had come over me. I sat staring into space for a while and doodling on my sketchbook with my charcoal crayon. The next part of my afternoon seemed stale, quiet and unproductive.

I couldn't help wondering why I had to bump into Trevor that day. I mean really what were the odds?

A million questions ran through my mind and dispersed through my ears – it was all I could think about for the best part of an hour. I kept trying to shake off my thoughts and continue with my work, but I found it difficult. I started to second guess myself and think about all of the good times Trevor and I once shared. I started to think about mum and how she was living up her best life in Taiwan and then I looked down and all I could see was my reality, a blank page with some scribble on it.

The questions that dispersed through my ears went in a circular motion and came back to infiltrate my mind. I started questioning myself and wondering whether I had just made a major mistake allowing Trevor to walk back out of my life again.

I finally shook myself out of that cycle and managed to draw a very minuscule sketch of a tree that was standing directly in front of me through the window. I couldn't focus on anything in the surrounding area, so I put all of my effort into sketching the oak tree. Then I stopped working again.

I went home that afternoon and I wrote another letter to God.

<u>Saturday 15th March</u>

Dear God,

I don't know how to feel right now.

When I saw Trevor today it knocked me back some years, I felt like I had been knocked back to my fifteen-year-old self once again. I know that I said all of the right things to Trevor, but I didn't feel them when I was saying them. I was thinking one thing and saying another.

When I told Trevor that I didn't want to swap numbers with him, I just said that because I knew it would be wrong, but on the inside, I wanted to say yes. As soon as Trevor left the café my mind went numb for a while – I started worrying and wondering about where he was going and whether or not he was with someone else. I found myself picturing Trevor's new girlfriend and wondering whether or not she was prettier than me.

I know that it's wrong of me to worry about these things because I read in the Bible that You said we shouldn't worry and that we should, 'be anxious for nothing ...' – Philippians 4:6.

I know that I shouldn't even be thinking about Trevor because he's not good for me, he's toxic. Right?

But God, I need You to help me and strengthen me in this situation. I regret saying no to Trevor earlier on today, I think that it would have been easier if I had just said yes! I don't know what to do now, I just need help.

Can You help me with my thoughts? God, I want to be strong. I want to be able to resist temptations and after I walk away. I want to be confident that I have made the right decision.

Kitsu xoxo

> " whatever things are true, whatever things are noble, whatever things are just, whatever things are pure, whatever things are lovely, whatever things are of good report, if there is any virtue and if there is anything praiseworthy — meditate on these things." — Philippians 4:8

I knew in that moment that if I was going to be free from my past, I mean really be free, then it was all going to have to start with me overcoming the negative thoughts in my mind. I knew that I would have to stop second-guessing every right decision that I made and stop thinking the worst about myself. I was going to have to focus my mind on things that were true and wonderful and admirable. I was going to have to think positive thoughts and be grateful for all of the good things that were going on in my life. I found a good friend in Bodel, but I found an even greater Friend in Jesus.

I AM Stronger Now

It was the summer after college, and I was confident that I had passed my English and Maths GCSE's and completed my Art and Design Apprenticeship. Shortly after taking my last exam, I started applying for universities; I got three conditional offers to go and study Architecture, this was based on me passing my Level 3 Apprenticeship and my GCSE retakes. I was sure that I had passed because this time I was focused, there were no distractions. I spent that year focusing on becoming a better version of myself. When I finished college in the summer, I was so contented with myself, I felt accomplished. I was on cloud nine.

That was the summer that I finally flew over to Taiwan to meet mum and her new husband. Yep, mum got married whilst she was out in Taiwan. She said she had to; it was something to do with her visa and eligibility to stay in the country. I didn't go to mums wedding though. I know it sounds selfish, but I just wasn't ready to think about her moving on with her life without me. I definitely wasn't moving to Taiwan any time soon. So, I stayed in London and focused on myself for a bit. I carried on writing letters to God just like Bodel told me to; through doing that I grew stronger and learnt so much about myself. Mum told me all about the wedding though. The time apart was good for us - mum and I that is.

By the time I finished college in the summer I was ready to face reality, I was ready to go and visit my mother and my stepfather. Saying the words 'step-father,' out loud without cringing was already a major step for me. When mum first told me that she had gotten married, I just remember a throbbing feeling in my neck, it was hard for me to swallow. It felt like mum had cut me out of her life. The time apart was good for us though, things felt different now. Mum was so ecstatic to hear that I was finally ready to come over and see them that she brought me a ticket for the first available date after college finished. I spent the majority of that fourteen-hour journey sleeping, but I did take some time out to contemplate what mum's new husband might be like. I wondered whether he would be anything like my dad. Not that I knew much about my dad, but I wondered what mum would look for in a man. She spent so much time telling me to be careful of these young boys, but I never got to know what kind of qualities mum would look for in a man. I didn't know what to expect, I had no idea what kind of man my mother would want to marry.

Mum's new husband was called Benjamin, his name was Benjamin Zou and he was a lawyer just like mum. I remember the first time I saw Benjamin. I had just stepped through the airport arrival doors; I was dragging my suitcase around the crowded airport terminal.

"Wait at the café on the corner."

That's what mum told me to do once I got through the arrival doors, she said that she and Benjamin would be waiting right next to the café on the corner. So, I dragged my suitcase past the queues of people, looking around frantically for this café on the corner. There were so many people in the airport that afternoon, perhaps they were waiting for their teenage daughter to come and meet their new husband for the very first time as well!

I couldn't find mum and Benjamin at first. I couldn't see the café on the corner either. Then all of a sudden, a tall, tanned skin man, with a tiny moustache walked up beside me. As I looked up, my heart felt warm. The man gazed down at me with glaring eyes. Don't ask me how I knew, but I knew in that moment it was him. That was mum's husband. That was Benjamin. Mum appeared by the other side of me, moments later. I could tell by the look on her face that she was pleased. I can't explain it, all I know is that when I saw mum and Benjamin together for the first time, fourteen hours - worth of anxious thoughts disappeared from my mind. Mum gave me a tight hug; Benjamin smiled at me and reached for my suitcase. He didn't drag my suitcase the way that I was dragging it and struggling intensely, he just kind of lifted it and carried it with one hand. Then we headed home.

Mum and Benjamin lived in a large, finely decorated modern house, in the capital city of Taiwan. They lived in a place called Taipei. It didn't take me too long to get to know Benjamin, he was kind, hospitable and had a sense of generosity about him. The more I got to know Benjamin, the more I began to understand why mum had chosen him. It was because he made her feel valued and worthwhile. All of the things that mum used to complain about, the things that she never got from my father. The recognition, the support, the appreciation - it was like mum had found all of those things in Benjamin. Seeing mum in Taiwan was like seeing a different person. I got it. I understood why mum was able to spend so much time out there without me, it's because she was trying to find herself just like I was. I guess I always thought of mum as just my mother, I didn't think about the things she may have wanted to accomplish within her own life as well. I guess I never really considered the fact that mum could've been lonely; perhaps she just wanted companionship. So many of my conversations with my mother were spent with her focusing on my life, and telling me what not to do. I finally got to see what she wanted for her own life. Mum just wanted to be accepted for who she was, she just wanted to feel like she belonged. These were the things that I found in Jesus and that's why I understood that mum had found her place in the huge complex place that we call life.

Mum thought that I had met someone new as well, so I told her that I did.

"There's something different about you, I just can't quite put my finger on it," Mum asked inquisitively one morning at breakfast. She asked; then she paused and waited. I told mum that I had met someone new. I told her that I had made a new friend at college called Bodel and she introduced me to Jesus.

"Jesus?" Mum asked me with a look devoid of expression. I couldn't untangle her thoughts.

I looked at mum with a straight face; I wanted her to see that what had happened to me was real.

"Yes mum, she introduced me to Jesus."

I told mum that I had been writing letters to God recently, and that I had been talking to Him about everything that was going on in my life.

"That's why I'm here mum," I continued that afternoon. "God helped me to realise that coming here was the right thing to do."

Mum didn't speak, she just listened. I continued.

"When I felt lost and rejected, God, helped me to see that I was accepted. I gave my life to Jesus mum. I'm born-again now."

Mum listened to me, she listened with sincerity; she could sense the genuineness in my voice. I was different, something had shifted in me. Mum smiled at me with intensity, I could tell by the glistening in her eyes that she understood everything that I was saying in that moment. Then, when I paused to take a breath, mum spoke.

"Yes sweetheart, and one day you will meet someone else who loves you, just like Jesus does."

Mum spoke to me with a voice of exhalation. It was like something she had been carrying around for years had been unstrapped from her chest and released. Mum was free and so was I.

I showed mum some of the letters that I had been writing to God. Mum seemed so delighted, she said that this was all she wanted, to see me happy.

"I tried to save you from so many things dear," mum began. "There comes a point where we have to just let go and look up. You know what I mean?"

I knew exactly what mum meant when she said that to me, and I was appreciative. I was grateful that mum left me to find my own feet and I was grateful that I could finally see things clearly. I could see what mum had been trying to tell me all of my life. In that moment I was still, and I was quiet, and I pondered for a moment. Then I was able to articulate my thoughts within my mind. There's a longing for love that many people have; we always try to fill it in with people and material things, but it never works, it never works because that fulfilment only comes from God.

I spent the first three weeks of my summer in Taiwan with mum and Benjamin. I could tell that mum was happy because I felt a peace in my heart before I left there to go back to London. Mum said that I could have the house to myself whilst she was away, and that she and Benjamin would come and visit me in London soon. Mum said that she trusted me to be as responsible as I had shown her that I could be all of this time.

Before I left Taiwan, mum did something I never expected.

It was our last evening in Taipei, Benjamin took mum and me out for dinner in a posh restaurant in a place called the Zhongshan District. Benjamin didn't eat with us though, he just dropped us there and came back later to take us home again. I think he wanted mum and I to spend some quality time together on our last evening. Whilst we were at dinner mum pulled out a crumpled-up piece of paper from her handbag and handed it over to me.

"What's this?" I asked with curiosity.

"Have a look," mum replied whilst looking at me intently.

I unfolded the crumpled piece of paper, not knowing what to expect. Then I saw the name 'Geoffrey Bolton' and a mobile telephone number written in the middle with blue ink.

"Geoffrey Bolton!" I exclaimed, whilst looking up at mum to see her reaction.

Mum stared at me for a while, a still, silent stare. She didn't say anything for a while so neither did I.

Finally, mum broke the tension with, "Your father has been asking of you."

She spoke to me in a calm neutral tone that didn't give me much to go by. Questions filled my mind but none of them came out of my mouth. I guess I was thinking, "Why now?"

I started to wonder at that moment, whether this was the first time my father had asked of me in all of these years.

"He just asked of me out of the blue?" I looked at mum awaiting a response.

Mum began to explain to me that he had contacted her about a year ago, but she was waiting for the right time to tell me. Mum explained why she waited, she didn't want my father to keep coming in and out of my life; that would do more harm than good. By this point in the conversation, I had crumpled the paper back up again and had been squeezing it tightly within the palms of my hands for the better part of ten minutes.

"What do I do with this now? I asked inquisitively.

"You hold on to it," mum replied.

I spoke but no words came out of my mouth.

'You contact him whenever you are ready," mum concluded with a smile.

I didn't know how to feel in that moment, so I just let the uneasiness linger in the air for a while. We carried on eating after that, we changed the subject and I told mum about my plans for the rest of the summer. This was all too much for me. I already knew what I was going to have to do as soon as I got home.

Friday 30th July

Dear God,

    Wow! So, my mum just took me out for dinner and turned my whole life upside down! What do I do God? What do I do? I mean who is Geoffrey Bolton anyway, right? I have not seen this man since I was six years old. That was almost fourteen years ago. He's practically a stranger!

    How can mum take me out for dinner and give me the phone number of an outright stranger? No! I'm not calling him. Ok, that's it. Rant over. I'll just take this crumpled piece of paper back to my mother in the morning.

Kitsu xoxo

The next morning, we were on our way to the airport, Benjamin, mum and I. I still had the crumpled paper with my father's number in a small compartment of my hand luggage. I was thinking about the best time to tell mum that I wasn't going to be calling him. Sitting on the back seat of the car, I waited patiently. That right time never actually came about. So, I didn't bring it up. I guess I realised I didn't need to say anything else to mum at that point. I mean she had told me that I could go ahead and contact my father whenever I was ready, it wasn't like there was any rush or any pressure to do anything. I decided to leave it. I wasn't going to end my trip to Taiwan with drama. Not that kind anyway.

The drop off at the airport was emotional. I didn't know when I was going to see mum again, living alone and having a house to yourself has its great perks but it does get lonely at times. Besides, spending so much time in Taiwan with mum brought back memories of the trips we took together when we were back in London. I remembered our coffee mornings at Costa and our lunch dates at Nando's in London Bridge. Then I thought about going back home to an empty house. It wasn't going to be for long I supposed. It was just for the summer until university started. Benjamin, Mum and I said our goodbyes at the airport. I didn't look back after the goodbye hug; I wanted the last image in my mind to be one of laughter and not of tears.

<u>Monday 2nd August</u>

Dear God,

It was good to see mum again; I'm glad that I finally got to meet Benjamin as well. I haven't seen mum this happy in a while. I pray for mum and Benjamin that their love will blossom and grow, and that they will keep You at the centre.

It's so weird that mum decided to give me dad's number all of a sudden; on my last day in Taiwan. Although, it was good that she was able to talk about him without complaining, it's almost like — she's been healed as well. I know that You're a healer because I can see that You healed her heart. You softened her heart towards my father. I pray that I will always hear Your voice and that I never stray far away from You.

I wonder how long dad has been asking of me for. God, I have no idea what I would say to my father if I saw him, I do want to get to know him it's just that I have no idea what to say to him — I haven't seen him for almost fourteen years. What does a daughter say to a father that she hasn't seen for almost fourteen years?

Kitsu xoxo

"Be kind to one another, tender-hearted, forgiving one another, as God in Christ forgave you." _ Ephesians 4:32

That Special Purpose

When I arrived at Heathrow airport the following afternoon, I was so tired I could barely feel my feet. I rolled myself out of the arrival gates, through passport control and down to the baggage claim area.

Sitting down on a metal bench near the baggage carousel, I began to rummage through my handbag. I was looking for something to keep myself occupied. I had £60 in my purse, that was the cash that Benjamin gave me to get a taxi home from the airport. Whilst I was glaring at the rolled-up £20 notes in my left hand, I made some quick calculations. It would cost about £60 to get a taxi from Heathrow to Peckham. However, that £60 could go towards something much more tangible if I just made a quick stopover at Oxford Street. Still sitting by the empty carousel, waiting for my luggage, I calculated that I could probably get two pairs of jeans from Top Shop or a smart blazer in Zara for that money. I wanted a new outfit for my first day at university anyway. All I had to do was take the Piccadilly line to Green Park; then change to the Jubilee Line and get off at Bond Street Station. Then I could walk down Oxford Street. My suitcase came onto the baggage carousel just at the right time. Only this time when I rolled it along the floor, it didn't seem so heavy anymore. So, I made a quick stop at Oxford Street on my way home from the airport. I brought a dark green, chequered blazer with leather elbow patches from Zara. I pictured myself wearing this blazer with some jeans and smart ankle boots on my first day at university.

As soon as I got home, I opened my front door; flung my suitcase on the floor and retreated to my bed. That was a nice holiday. That wasn't all that happened to me that summer, I had so much good news it was overwhelming, it was one of the greatest summers of my life.

The following morning, I woke up and opened up my mail. I was ecstatic to find out that I had gotten offers from all of the universities that I applied to that year. In particular, I got a scholarship to study Architecture at the Manchester School of Architecture.

Everything was going so well. I knew that my faith in God was going to be tested again soon; I was ready. Trevor was back in London for the holidays and I knew it was only a matter of time before I bumped into him again.

Then it happened one Sunday afternoon. Bodel and I had gone out for lunch in the West End after church. I was telling Bodel about my time in Taiwan with mum. She was telling me that she was on her way back from France - that's where her father lived so she went to go and visit him. I told Bodel that mum had given me my father's number recently as well and also that I didn't know what to say to him. I wanted to contact him, but I just didn't know what to say. Bodel responded with something that shocked me.

"But have you forgiven him though? That's the real question."

"What do you mean?" I inquired of her.

"I mean exactly what I said," Bodel reiterated.

This question made me pause and ponder for a moment, I never really asked myself that question. I had to think. Perhaps it wasn't a case of not knowing what to say to my father. Perhaps the real question was whether or not I had forgiven him. I thought I had forgiven him, but then I second-guessed myself. I paused and looked at Bodel for a moment.

"I have forgiven him," saying it aloud made it seem just that tiny bit more real.

"I've forgiven my father," I said this with a slight crack in my voice, it was almost like an uncertainty mixed with a truth that I so desperately wanted to be real. Denial is a promise blocker.

Bodel sat and looked at me, she didn't say much, she let me speak for a while. We were sat down in a nice little outdoor café on the corner of Regent Street. Watching the steam rise up from my creamy cup of mocha, searching through my memories, it was there that I came to the realisation that moving forward starts with letting go. Bodel told me that to move forward I would have to make peace with my past. I would have to forgive my father and let go of the pain and the hurt that was caused by his abandonment of me. Calling it abandonment was an enormous step for me; that's what it was though. Dad didn't just leave mum because they weren't getting along anymore, he abandoned me as well. So, I knew at that moment that I had to forgive my father for abandoning me.

That's when it happened, on the brink of that conversation, that's when it happened again.

That's where we saw him, that's where we saw Trevor. He was walking with a slim, fair-skinned lady and his arm was wrapped tightly around her waist. She had a tiny, yellow Selfridges bag in her right hand and a tall, plastic, Starbucks cup in her left. I didn't recognise her. She didn't look like anyone I had seen before; I don't think she was from our school or anything. I assumed that she was Trevor's girlfriend. Trevor and his girlfriend were with a toddler. The child looked about four years old. I know that Trevor saw us; this time he seemed quite hesitant about stopping and coming over to the table where we were sitting. I carried on looking at him. I didn't turn away, so they stopped and walked in our direction. I felt my heart sink a little bit lower than usual, but I still looked at Trevor refusing to withdraw my stance.

"Hi Trevor," I began.

"Hey, Kitsu how you doing?" Trevor continued.

Trevor wasn't his usual loud and obnoxious self, there was a certain level of humility that hovered alongside his greeting this time around.

I looked at Trevor's girlfriend and the child, but I didn't say anything to them. I said it with my eyes though and I know that Trevor sensed it too.

The glint in my eye said, "Are you not going to introduce us then?"

Trevor replied in a seemingly nervous manner.

"This is my girlfriend Caroline, and this is my...this is my son Kayden."

Trevor hesitated as he spoke, he looked down because he knew what he was saying. He was telling me that he was lying; he was lying to me all of those years ago when he said he hadn't been cheating on me. He was lying when he said that I could trust him. But what did it matter now anyway? It didn't.

"Nice to meet you, Caroline," I replied with a straight expression on my face.

I looked at Caroline, but I couldn't see any resemblance between her and Kayden. He looked completely different from both of them. I didn't ask any more questions after that. What did it matter, right? What did it matter what Trevor had been up to? All I knew at that moment was that I had escaped. I came face to face with the truth. I had almost thrown my whole life away for a fantasy; a fairy-tale life with Trevor that never existed anywhere outside of my teenage imagination. I wondered for a moment what else Trevor had been lying to me about.

Then I paused and I remembered who I was.

So that was it, Bodel looked at me; smiled, then we turned our attention back to our conversation. I watched Trevor walk away that day and I didn't think about him again. I didn't feel any resentment towards him, I just felt a sadness mixed with gratitude. The thought that our whole relationship had been a lie brought an element of sadness but that was further soothed by the gratitude in knowing that I had been set free.

Bodel and I went to church later on that evening; we had a special service with a visiting preacher from Atlanta, Georgia. Ironically, he was preaching a sermon about love – the Father's love. I remember him saying, that God looks at us as His children. All those who receive Jesus into their lives, all those who believe in His name, God gives the right to become children of God.

Sunday 15th August

Dear God,

Thank you for showing me the truth, You have shown me the truth about my past and the truth about my future. I know who I am now – I am Yours.

Seeing Trevor with his new girlfriend and his child wasn't as difficult as I thought it would be, I mean I guess when I asked You to heal me and set me free from the past, I wasn't expecting to find out something like that. I don't feel heart-broken though, there was a time in my life when finding out the truth about Trevor would have broken me. It would have shattered me straight into a state of depression. But not anymore, not this time. I guess I'm just relieved.

Yes, I am relieved, and I am grateful.

Thank you for not allowing me to throw my whole life away for a boy that didn't even care about me. I'm grateful that You taught me how to love myself. You showed me the true meaning of love by sending Your Son Jesus Christ to die on the cross for our sins. Wow! Thank you for healing me and opening my eyes God. Thank you for helping me to see myself the way that You see me.

Kitsu xoxo

"I will be a Father to you, And you shall be My
sons and daughters, Says the Lord Almighty."
– 2 Corinthians 6:18 "For we are His workmanship,
created in Christ Jesus for good works, which God prepared
beforehand that we should walk in them." – Ephesians 2:10

So that's how God began to break down the wall. He broke it down with His words. Those words pierced through my inner being like a double-edged sword, they scraped away at my fears and broke through the pain of my rejection. They spoke to my small, minuscule pieces and started to mend them back together again. Overwhelmed, my heart was full, I cried so much that evening. The tears dripped through the corners of my eyes and soaked into my pillow, but these weren't tears of brokenness they were tears of happiness and joy. After I had finally digested the words that God spoke to me through His Word, I grabbed a hold of my duvet; threw it over my head and fell into a deep, peaceable sleep. I fell asleep thinking about the things I wish I knew when I was fifteen years old.

The next morning, I woke up with my Bible on my pillow next to me. I opened it up and immediately, my eyes fell onto a snippet of the words that I had read the night before – 'God's workmanship.' As an art student and an aspiring architect, those words jumped out at me; it was the language of construction.

God calls me 'His workmanship.' When He says this, He is reminding me that He is the manufacturer and that I am His skilfully, crafted, hand-made design.

God wants us to know that we are valuable to Him; we are His work of art. God created us to accomplish great things for Him, things that He prepared in advance of us coming to know Him. This means that we have a special purpose in Christ Jesus. Now I'm looking forward to that special purpose.

Kitsu xoxo

Printed in the United States
By Bookmasters